They were taking him back to civilisation beneath a winter moon. Soon he would be with Sallie. He was desperate for the sight of her, the smell of her.

She heard his key in the lock a second before the phone rang and, ignoring its strident interruption, she flew down the stairs and into his arms. For an endless moment they stood entwined in the bliss of being together again, shaken by the depth of their feelings.

When she looked up she was weeping, and he said softly, 'Don't cry, Sal.' At that the tears flowed faster.

'Hey,' he chided. 'I'm back, safe and sound.'

'I thought I was going to lose you, and I'd never told you that I love you, now more than ever. I love you for the way you've tried so hard to make up for what you did. For the way you are such a clever, caring doctor.' She was smiling now. 'And because you are still the most attractive and the sexiest of men.'

His smile was brighter than the sun. 'Is that so?' he breathed. 'I'll see if I can live up to that...'

Abigail Gordon loves to write about the fascinating combination of medicine and romance from her home in a Cheshire village. She is active in local affairs, and is even called upon to write the script for the annual village pantomime! Her eldest son is a hospital manager and helps with all her medical research. As part of a close-knit family, she treasures having two of her sons living close by, and the third one not too far away. This also gives her the added pleasure of being able to watch her delightful grandchildren growing up.

THE VILLAGE DOCTOR'S MARRIAGE

BY
ABIGAIL GORDON

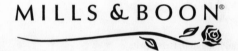

MILLS & BOON®

First published in Great Britain 2006
Harlequin Mills & Boon Limited,
Eton House, 18-24 Paradise Road, Richmond, Surrey TW9 1SR

© Abigail Gordon 2006

ISBN-13: 978 0 263 19518 7
ISBN-10:   0 263 19518 X

Set in Times Roman 10½ on 13½ pt
15-1106-48508

Printed and bound in Great Britain
by Antony Rowe Ltd, Chippenham, Wiltshire

THE VILLAGE DOCTOR'S MARRIAGE

CHAPTER ONE

SALLIE BEAUMONT was smiling as she stopped her car on the forecourt of the village medical practice. It was a bright spring morning and everywhere had been bursting into life as she'd visited those who hadn't been well enough to attend the surgery.

There'd been splashes of colour in cottage gardens, fresh green leaves on the trees, and the sun beaming down onto the place that was so dear to her heart was like a blessing from the serene heavens.

She was always happy to see the end of winter. The loneliness was easier to cope with on bright days, instead of on dull afternoons and long dark nights. But that was the last thing on her mind today.

Part of the huge gap in her life was about to be filled. A temporary arrangement maybe, but for the next six months there would be a child in the apartment above the practice, the baby of a single mother who had been offered the chance of a lifetime that she couldn't afford to miss. But it was going to mean leaving her baby behind.

A niece of Sallie's by marriage, Melanie had become

pregnant while in a disastrous relationship that had foundered once the father-to-be had realised the score. The country doctor had known nothing about it until there'd been a phone call one day to say that the twenty-one-year-old was in hospital having given birth to a baby boy, and would she like to visit? She hadn't needed to be asked twice, and it had been the beginning of a friendship that had deepened as the weeks had gone by.

The girl's parents had died some time previously and until Sallie had appeared on the scene she'd had no one to turn to. But Melanie was a fighter, independent, ready to take a risk, and when she'd been offered a six-month contract as a dancer in a show in America, she'd asked Sallie if she would have little Liam until she came back.

'You know I love dancing,' she'd coaxed. 'It's my life, Sallie. I've trained, worked at it, and dreamt of something like this turning up, but I couldn't leave my baby with anyone else but you.'

'I don't have to be persuaded,' Sallie had told her. 'Of course I'll look after Liam, and between Hannah and myself, we'll cope. She loves children, too. We'll take good care of him.'

And today was the day when the lonely apartment above the surgery was going to come to life. Melanie was bringing Liam round that evening and flying out to New York in the morning, and every time Sallie thought about it she found herself smiling. There hadn't been much to smile about in her life over the last three years, but this *was* something to be happy about.

However, before that there was the late afternoon

surgery to get through. She would be taking one and Colin Carstairs, the senior partner at the practice, the other. He had seemed distracted of late, and when he'd seen off the last of his patients he came into her room and perched himself on the corner of her desk.

She looked up enquiringly and he said casually, 'Do you ever hear from that husband of yours, Sallie?'

'I had a card from Steve at Christmas,' she told him, startled by the question.

'Where is he based these days?'

'I don't know. It had a Gloucester postmark on the envelope. The year before it was Cornwall. The year before that London. So it would seem that he's moving about all the time. But why do you ask?'

He answered her question with another of his own. 'How would you feel about him coming back into the practice, if he was willing?'

How would she feel? How would she feel if the only man she'd ever loved came back into her life. It wasn't an easy question to answer. She would be eager to see him again, but apprehensive after the way they'd parted, and not prepared to have her life torn apart again when she'd done nothing wrong.

But Steve was proud and stubborn. Whatever it was that Colin had in mind, she couldn't see Steve coming back after all this time unless he had got over his despair.

'When the pair of you joined the practice, I thought it was my birthday,' Colin was saying. 'Two young graduates, husband and wife, keen and able. Stephen was a like a flash of light around the place and you were his anchor.'

Not any more, she thought miserably.

'Why are we on this subject?' she asked flatly. 'And why would you want Steve back in the practice? I know we are very busy but—'

'Jess and I are moving to Canada.'

'What?'

'You know that David and his family are out there and they are forever trying to persuade us to join them. Needless to say, Jessica is pining for her grandchildren so we're going to take the plunge. I know I'm only in my late fifties, but I feel ready to retire and enjoy the good life.'

Then Colin sighed and patted her hand. 'But, Sallie, I don't want to go and leave you coping with some stranger. You are the best, and so is Stephen. The village folk love and respect you and if he came back they would be well suited. But how about you? How would you feel?'

'I would have mixed feelings,' she said with a strained smile. 'He's the only man I've ever loved and nothing is going to change that, but apart from the Christmas cards he hasn't been in touch in three years. That would take some forgiving and, in any case, how do you know he would want to come back?'

'I don't. But there's no harm in asking.'

Her heartbeat was thudding in her ears. His parting words had always prevented *her* from doing that. 'Forget about me, Sal,' he'd said harshly. 'I need some space. Find yourself some other guy who can give you children.'

'I don't want anyone else,' she'd cried above the noise of the car engine on a dark November night. 'I only want you.' But he hadn't heard her and she knew he wouldn't have changed his mind if he had. As far as Steve had been concerned, he'd wanted out.

'So it's all right with you if I put out some feelers?' Colin was asking. 'I don't want to cause him any embarrassment by going through official channels to locate him. I have a friend who practises in the Gloucester area. I'll give him a ring and let you know if I come up with anything as I'm not going to Canada until I've spoken to Steve.'

'Yes, whatever you say,' she agreed weakly, and, gathering up her belongings, she went upstairs.

As he'd watched her go Colin had thought that for once the practice wasn't his main concern. He was using it as an excuse to try and bring two people that he held in high regard back into each other's lives.

If ever he'd thought a marriage solid it had been theirs. They'd adored each other until the time that Stephen had seen one of his most precious dreams put in jeopardy and Sallie had been faced with the painful fact that her loving support was not enough.

He, Colin, was looking forward to the new life that he and his wife were planning, but felt that before he went he had to try to bring about a reconciliation between Sallie and Stephen.

It had been three years since Stephen had left the practice and he had watched Sallie cope with her misery as best she could. She had been blameless. Ready to support her clever, impatient husband in every way. But he'd still gone, and if he hadn't met anyone else, or put down roots somewhere, maybe he might have calmed down and be ready to see sense. But first he had to find him.

Colin's revelation that he wanted Steve back in the practice before he went to Canada had been a week ago, and as she waited for him to come up with some news of him, the only thing that was saving Sallie's sanity was Melanie's baby.

At two months Liam was a contented little mite with soft golden down on his head and eyes as blue as a summer sky. Every time she held him Sallie knew how much she ached for children of her own, but they would have to be Steve's children, too, and the likelihood of that was remote, due to the long-term effects of his illness and the fact that she would be wary of having her heart broken again.

Theirs had been the happiest of marriages until he'd been diagnosed with testicular cancer and everything had begun to fall apart. For one thing, the timing of it had been catastrophic. It had come when he had been desperate for them to start a family. So much so that it had caused difficulties in their relationship because she'd wanted to wait a while, having worked hard to get where she was, and in that unsettled state of affairs had come the cancer. She had supported him all the way, but it seemed it hadn't been enough. Instead of bringing them closer, it had driven them apart and in the end, after months of angry frustration on Steve's part, he had gone and she hadn't seen him since.

* * *

Hannah Morrison had been their housekeeper ever since they'd arrived in the village eight years ago and was a plump, motherly, sixty-year-old. Her children were now leading their own lives, and Hannah looked after Sallie as if she were one of them.

When she'd been told about the baby coming to live in the apartment above the surgery, she'd smiled her delight. It would be like the old days, having a wee mite to cuddle, she'd said, and thought that it would give the lonely doctor something to love. The housekeeper often wondered how Sallie kept so calm with no husband, no children and a busy practice always making demands on her. She never once complained.

In the week since Liam's arrival Sallie had developed a routine. Up early to give him his six o'clock bottle, then, when she'd had her breakfast, it was bathtime. When Hannah arrived at just before half past eight she was ready to take off the mantle of stand-in mother and become the village doctor, reverting back again once the late surgery was over.

She was loving every minute of it, but at the back of her mind all the time was the thought of Colin trying to find Steve and what might, or might not, come of it. He hadn't mentioned it since, and she wondered if he'd given up on the idea.

He would tell her if she asked, but every time she thought of it her insides began to churn. If Steve came back, what would it be like? They'd been apart for such a long time.

There had been a lot of interest among the village

folk when the news had got around that the doctor was looking after someone else's baby. Some said it was a pity it wasn't her own and what was Stephen Beaumont playing at? The reason for his departure had never been general knowledge. Colin had protected Sallie from the gossip as much as he'd been able to, and gradually it had died down.

It was six o'clock, Hannah had just left and after a busy day in the practice Sallie was feeding Liam when there was a ring at the side door downstairs that led to the apartment. Hannah must have forgotten something, she thought.

Lifting Liam up into her arms, she placed the bottle on to the table, and as he began to howl in protest she carried him carefully down the steep staircase that led to the surgery below. There was a smile on her face as she unlocked the door, but it was wiped off by sheer amazement as she saw that Hannah hadn't forgotten anything.

Steve was standing on the mat, and as the shock of seeing him hit her she clutched the baby to her and took a step back.

'Hello, Sallie,' he said, as she stood transfixed in front of him. 'Can I come in?'

Speechless, she moved to one side to let him pass and as he brushed against her the dark, compelling gaze that she knew so well was fixed on the baby.

'I see you did as I suggested,' he said levelly. 'Found someone who could give you a child.'

She was adjusting to the shock of seeing him. Her mind

was working again, her speech coming back. Pointing to the staircase, she suggested, 'If you'd like to go up.'

'After you,' he said in the same tone, and, still holding the crying baby tightly in her arms, she led the way.

'As usual, you're jumping to the wrong conclusions,' she said quietly, as the hurt that his opening comment had caused settled around her heart.

He was standing in the middle of the sitting room, looking around him, and raised a dark eyebrow. 'In what way?'

'Liam isn't mine. He belongs to *your* niece, Melanie, who was living with some guy who disappeared when he discovered she was pregnant. At present she's working in America and I'm looking after her baby for her.'

'What? She should have come to me. You shouldn't be lumbered with my family's problems,' he exclaimed.

'Oh, yes? There would have been the small matter of Melanie having to find you first, and I am not being lumbered at all. Liam is adorable and I love having him.'

Trying to stay calm, she picked up Liam's bottle and started to feed the now quiet infant. She could feel Steve's gaze on her and decided to change the subject.

'So why are you here, Steve?' she asked coolly. 'Has Colin been in touch?'

He went to stand by the window and looked out onto the village and the peaks beyond. 'Not with me, but a colleague of mine told me he was looking for me. So I decided to come and find out why.'

After the way he'd behaved in the past, he couldn't face telling Sallie that when he'd heard Colin was seeking him out, he'd immediately thought that there was something wrong with her and he'd come rushing from Gloucestershire in fear and dread, only to be faced with the sickening anticlimax of her appearing in front of him with a baby in her arms. And as usual he'd been too quick off the mark with what he'd said when he'd seen it.

He'd heard a baby crying as he'd rung the doorbell, but had thought it came from outside the practice building rather than inside. When she'd opened the door with the crying infant in her arms, he'd felt as if someone had struck him a hard blow to the chest.

Sallie was taking in every detail of him now that she'd got used to the shock of his arrival. He looked older, tired, as if his batteries needed recharging. The long, lean length of him was thinner, the dark pelt of his hair seemed to have lost its gloss, but he was still a man who would stand out among other men. A man that women looked at twice, some of them three times, and once he had been hers.

Legally he still was. Neither of them had ever filed for divorce and incredibly he was here, back where he belonged, but not because of her. He'd come to see what Colin wanted of him and would probably turn on his heel and go back to where he'd come from once he knew.

'So what does Colin want me for?' he asked, as his gaze moved again to the countryside that he had loved as much as she did.

'He and Jessica are going to live in Canada and he wants you to come back into the practice so that he can leave with an easy mind.'

His heart was leaping with thankfulness as he listened

to what she had to say. A way to make amends to her was opening out before him, but he wasn't going to let her see his joy, not yet. Sallie might not want him back in her life and if that *was* the case, who could blame her?

'I'm surprised to hear that after the way I went storming off,' he said dryly.

She knew this man, Sallie was thinking. Knew him better than she knew herself. Knew his virtues and his failings, and when it came to those, pride was top of the list.

'He understood in part what you did. So did I. But I had more to lose than Colin had, much more. But, Steve, this isn't the time to talk about that. It isn't about us. It's about the practice. I've learned to cope without you, so don't let what happened between us affect your decision when he asks you.'

'So you aren't bothered whether I come back or not.'

Liam had finished his feed and was ready to be burped, and as she raised him gently upright she told Steve, 'It would be good for the practice if you did. Colin says you were the best, and I agree. I'm sure the patients would be pleased to see you back.'

And she would be walking on a tightrope she thought, afraid of falling off and finding herself back where she had been when Steve had left her. But she reminded herself that he hadn't travelled from Gloucestershire on her account. Curiosity had brought him, and if anyone could persuade him to rejoin the practice, it was the man who was about to depart from it.

'Colin has gone home,' she told him. 'He locked up

down below and left just before you arrived, but I know he'd love you to go and see him.'

'I suppose I might as well hear what he has to say now that I'm here,' he said with assumed easiness.

'Where are you working at the moment?' she asked. If it was something challenging and exciting, he wasn't going to want to come back to country life.

'I've been doing some floating around as a locum. Killing time, really, until I found something that I wanted to stick with.'

'So you didn't veer off into a hospital environment.'

'I thought of it, but general practice is what I do best. So I'll pop round to see Colin and no doubt he'll let you know the outcome of our meeting.'

It was the outcome of *their* meeting that she was concerned about, she thought painfully. From what Steve had just said, he didn't intend calling back after he'd seen the senior partner, which didn't sound hopeful.

'Bye, Sallie,' he said at the door. 'Take care of yourself and Liam.'

She nodded and turned away. It had been on the tip of her tongue to say that the comment was somewhat overdue. That she'd had a lot of practice at taking care of herself.

From the window she watched him go, driving towards Colin's house and out of her life again. Once his car was out of sight, reaction began to set in and she felt weak and disorientated. If anyone had told her an hour ago that Steve would be standing in that very room before the night was out she would have laughed.

As the minutes ticked by she found herself wandering from room to room. Was Steve still with Colin? she wondered. Or had their meeting been brief and he was on his way back to Gloucestershire? Would the senior partner let her know what had been decided tonight, or leave it until the morning?

She made a meal but couldn't eat it. When the doorbell rang a second time she ran down the stairs and flung the door open, but it wasn't Steve on the step this time. It was Colin, observing her with a satisfied expression.

'He's coming back, Sallie,' he said. 'What do you think about that?'

'To be honest, I don't know,' she breathed. 'Are you happy about it?'

'Yes, I'm delighted. He didn't need much persuading. Said he's been working in inner cities since he left and has really missed village life. He'll have to fulfil his commitment to the practice where he's working at present and will join us in a month's time.'

So he'd missed village life, but not his *village wife,* she thought wryly. But at least he was going to be where she could see him every day, talk to him, even if it was only about the patients. Would he want to come back to the apartment or find a place of his own? she wondered as her mind leapt from one possibility to another.

'You *are* happy about it, aren't you, Sallie?' Colin asked.

'Yes, of course I am. You've created an opportunity for Steve and I to put things right between us, Colin, and I thank you for it. But I have to say it won't be easy.

Three years is a long sentence for someone who did nothing wrong.'

'Yes. I know, my dear,' he said gravely. 'All I can say to that is Steve was in deep despair, and me asking him to come back is because I hate to see you apart when you had such a good marriage. If his return should prove that it is mendable, I will be a happy man. I want the best for the practice, but I want to see the two of you back together even more.'

When Colin had gone, Sallie sank down onto the sofa and tried to sort out her thoughts. She had come alive during the last few hours. The husband she'd loved more than life itself had appeared at her door and she was still in shock. But what had happened to them wasn't going to be wiped out like a bad dream. It would always be there. She could live with it, but if Steve hadn't moved on during their separation there wasn't really anything to rejoice about.

He had told her to find someone else who could give her children on that never-to-be-forgotten night when he'd driven out of her life, but he'd still been uptight at seeing her with Liam in her arms. It had been there in his glance for the briefest of seconds and then it had gone.

She went into the bedroom and stood looking down at the sleeping baby. 'I've seen Steve today, Liam,' she told him. 'He was near enough to touch. He looks older, tired, yet the magnetism is still there. But I am not going to let him hurt me again...ever.'

There was no comment forthcoming, just a windy little smile that said all was right with *his* world.

* * *

While Sallie's had been wistful thoughts about the past, Steve's were very much in the future as he drove back to his rented flat in a busy market town in the Midlands.

Colin's proposal that he rejoin the practice and run it jointly with Sallie had opened the doors that he, Steve, had shut behind him in the trauma of three years ago. He was being given a second chance and hadn't needed to be asked twice.

This was where he belonged, he'd thought. In the beautiful Cheshire village that he should never have left in the first place. Here Sallie would be back in his life again. Not as before maybe. He didn't deserve that, but he would be able to see her, speak to her and work with her once more.

He would have liked to have gone back to the apartment and told her himself that he'd agreed to Colin's suggestion. It would have been another opportunity to see her, if only briefly. A chance to gauge just how enthusiastic she was going to be about the new arrangement, but common sense had said it would be pushing it, foisting himself onto her twice in one day.

She hadn't given a straight answer when he'd asked how she would feel about him coming back, and he could hardly blame her for that. She'd almost dropped the baby when she'd seen him standing on the doorstep, while he had immediately thought wretchedly that he'd left it too late.

When she'd told him the child wasn't hers he had sent up a silent prayer of thanks. It had been followed by another when he'd heard what Colin had to say. And now he was going back to the place where he'd worked for the last nine months to tie up loose ends and prepare for the move, and if it meant waiting a few more weeks before he saw Sallie again, he could endure it. Compared to three years, it would be like a moment in time.

Colin had suggested that instead of he and Jessica putting their house up for sale, Steve could rent it if he wished. He'd hesitated. For one thing it was a large family house and a family was something he hadn't got. And for another, if there was the slightest chance of Sallie being prepared to have him back in the apartment, he wouldn't want to miss out on *that*.

'Think it over for a couple of weeks,' the senior partner had said. 'You've made the most important decision—the rest will fall into place.'

The practice side of it might, he'd thought wryly. But his marriage wasn't going to suddenly resurrect itself, and he had only himself to blame for that.

He'd gone to the local garage to fill up the petrol tank before setting off on the return journey and had seen another face from the past at the petrol pumps.

Anna Gresty and her husband had a farm on the road that led out of the village. When he'd been around previously it had been a prosperous, well-run establishment with a farm shop and stables. But from what she'd had to tell him, life was not now so good for the Grestys.

After she'd expressed her pleasure at the sight of him and been even more pleased to hear that he was coming back to work in the practice, Anna had told him soberly that her husband, Philip, was no longer the fit man that he'd been. That he'd been diagnosed with motor neurone disease and the illness was taking its toll.

The two men had been good friends. With no parents of his own, Steve had felt that the burly farmer had filled the gap that the loss of his father had left, and sometimes they'd gone walking together or played golf.

He'd been desperately sorry to hear that his friend had succumbed to something so debilitating and had told Anna, 'I'll be back permanently in just a few weeks' time and that man of yours will be my first priority. Who's been looking after him, Colin or Sallie?'

'He's been one of Colin's patients,' she'd told him.

'And Colin is moving away, so now Philip will be mine.' He smiled. 'Well, I need to get going, but it was good to see you. Tell Philip I'll see him soon.'

'Take care, Steve.'

'You, too, Anna,' he'd replied, and after giving her a swift kiss on the cheek he'd driven away from the pumps and out onto the road that led to the motorway.

Anna hadn't asked about Sallie and he was glad. Time enough for that when he knew where he stood with his wife. The news about Philip had brought him up with a jolt, taken the edge off his elation. It was another stick to beat himself with, that he hadn't been there for the man when he'd needed him

It was gone midnight when he arrived back at the drab flat that had been his home over recent months, and Steve had already decided that if he wasn't going to see

Sallie again until the date of the transfer, he was going to allow himself the pleasure of hearing her voice again. But it would have to wait until the morning as she would almost certainly be asleep.

He rang early the next day. When she answered he could hear the baby crying in the background and asked, 'What's wrong with Liam?'

'Nothing,' she told him coolly. 'Except that he's just woken up and wants his breakfast. So what do you want, Steve?' Now there was a chill in her voice.

He winced at the other end of the line. He'd got off on the wrong foot again by mentioning the baby.

'I'm phoning to ask if Colin has told you that I've agreed to come back and share the running of the practice with you.'

'Yes, he's told me.'

'And?'

'Better the devil one knows, I suppose,' she said with the same lack of warmth.

'I see,' he said slowly. 'So I'm going to be tolerated. I was going to ask if I could move back into the apartment, on a strictly business arrangement, of course, and only if you're comfortable with it. Colin has offered me his house to rent and I've told him I'll think about it, but it would be easier from a working point of view if I was based above the surgery.'

Sallie slumped down onto the chair near the phone. She felt as if her legs were going to give way. He hadn't changed, she was thinking. No sooner the thought than the deed. But he was going to have to stew for a while.

Steve had returned to the village out of curiosity, because he'd heard Colin was looking for him. He hadn't come back because he couldn't stay away from her any longer. So far there had been no mention of the day when he'd turned her life into a mere existence.

Surely he didn't think that by coming back he had blotted it out. She had cried into her pillow for nights on end and exhausted herself in the daytime, coping with the gap he'd left in the practice, and now it felt that he was contemplating returning as if nothing had happened.

There was silence at the other end of the line and Steve thought he'd blown it. Why couldn't he have waited a few days before asking if he could come back to live in the apartment? Yet he'd known all along that if he ever saw Sallie again he would be lost. That the firm resolve that had kept him from her would disappear, and he hadn't been wrong. He wanted her back with every fibre of his being and he was going the wrong way about it. Sounding pushy and confident when he was feeling anything but.

'I'd have to have a long think on that one,' she was saying into the silence. 'I've got used to living on my own. One can get used to anything in time. And now I have Liam to brighten my days. It's only temporary, but it would be a strange set-up, an estranged husband and wife living under the same roof with someone else's baby.'

'All right,' he agreed. 'Whatever you say. I'll probably tell Colin that I'll accept his offer to rent his house.'

The baby was exercising his lungs again and Sallie said, 'I'll have to go, Steve. I'll be in touch when I've given your suggestion some thought.'

'Fair enough,' he said. 'Bye for now, Sal.'

As she put the phone down her eyes were awash with tears. Theirs had been the strangest of separations. There'd been no one else involved, just the two of them…and cancer.

Steve had been strong and resilient and had tried to take it in his stride. But when it had affected his chances of fatherhood, he had hit rock bottom.

CHAPTER TWO

COLIN and Jessica were leaving to start their new life in Canada on a Saturday in June. Four weeks had gone by since Steve had first arrived back in the village and now he was due to return on Sunday in readiness to take over his position in the practice on Monday morning. As the days had gone by, each one bringing nearer the moment of his arrival, Sallie had tried to keep calm.

Fortunately Liam took up a lot of her free time, which gave her less opportunity to question what was happening to her. He was filling out and becoming aware of the world around him, with little toothless smiles for herself and Hannah.

She kept thinking how bizarre it was that Steve, who so desperately wanted children, should come back into her life when she was caring for Melanie's baby, and the fact that she'd offered him the spare room if he wanted it was going to complicate matters even more.

But as she'd told him when she'd rung to let him know her decision, the apartment was as much his as hers and the room was there if he wanted it. That had been all she'd said, but the message had been clear. He would not be sleeping in her bed, much as she ached to feel him close once more.

'Fine, Sal,' he'd said immediately. 'It really will be more convenient to live above the surgery but only if you're sure.'

He was the only person who'd ever called her Sal and when she'd said a cool goodbye she had wished he wouldn't. The name belonged to the past. To the good days when they'd lived for each other. Before circumstances had changed out of all recognition the husband she'd adored.

When she said goodbye to Colin he'd hugged her and told her, 'I hope I haven't done the wrong thing in bringing Steve back into your life, Sallie.'

She shook her head. 'No. I needed this, Colin. It is a second chance and if it doesn't work out, this time at least I'll have closure. I've lived in a miserable sort of limbo ever since he went and that isn't how I want to spend the rest of my days.'

And now it was Sunday evening. Steve had phoned to say that he was on his way and would be arriving in the village within the hour.

'Your great-uncle Stephen is coming home,' she told Liam as she bent over his cot and watched his golden lashes drooping. He gave a sleepy smile and she thought how her small charge was completely unaware of the significance of the moment. He had a full stomach and a dry bottom and was ready to sleep.

A ring on the doorbell told her that the moment had arrived and she went downstairs quickly to let him in. Her heartbeat was quickening and her face flushed as she faced him in the doorway. It was like it had been on that night a month ago when she'd opened the door to him, but this time she already knew who would be standing there.

So far neither of them had spoken. Steve was holding a suitcase in each hand and observing her with an expression that told her nothing. 'Is there anything else you need to bring in?' she croaked.

'No,' he told her. 'I was in rented accommodation and travel light. How are you?'

'I'm all right,' she replied quietly, and led the way upstairs.

He was looking around him. 'Where's Liam?'

'Asleep in his cot in my room,' she told him. 'I don't expect you'll hear much of him during the night. He sleeps right through now.'

She was gabbling like a nervous schoolgirl, she thought, and had no reason to. Steve was the one who should be ill at ease. He looked pale but composed and she said, 'Have you eaten?'

He observed her blankly as if she was speaking a foreign language. 'I'm all right. I had a bacon sandwich at midday. But I wouldn't mind a cuppa.' He moved towards the spare room and paused in the doorway, then went in and put the suitcases down.

She'd had the room redecorated, emptied the wardrobe, bought new bed linen, and all the time hadn't been able to believe she was doing it for Steve. But as proof that she *had* been doing it for him, he was there, throwing his jacket onto the bed and turning towards her like a guest who had just arrived for a short stay.

If he'd held out his arms she would have found it difficult not to have gone into them like a homing bird, but he didn't. He merely said, as a guest might have, 'The room looks nice. I see you've changed the colour scheme.'

She nodded unsmilingly, and followed it by saying, 'I'll go and put the kettle on while you unpack.' And without giving him the chance to come out with any more trivialities, she hurried into the kitchen, filled the kettle and then leaned limply against the units.

His unpacking couldn't have taken long as by the time she'd gathered her wits and was making him a sandwich, Steve appeared in the doorway and stood watching her with a dark, inscrutable sort of concentration that had her faltering in her task.

'If that is for me, thanks,' he said. 'But I don't want you to feel you have to feed me. I'll see to myself.'

Sallie slowly put the knife down. 'I don't intend waiting on you. But If you are suggesting we eat separately, forget it, Steve. I know what you like and you know what I like, so I suggest we take turns. One day I'll fix the meals and the next you can do it. There's also Liam to feed and that can be time-consuming.'

'Fine.' Steve nodded. 'So when it's your turn to

prepare our meals, I'll feed him. How about that, as you seem to be in favour of us eating together?'

'It is merely a matter of what is easiest and quickest, that's all,' she said evenly. 'Making the best of a bad job. Once you've had a drink and a bite, maybe we could discuss practice matters. This time tomorrow you'll have spent your first day back in the surgery. But before we talk there is just one thing.' She met his gaze. 'Is it going to upset you, having Liam in such close proximity? I know how you…'

'Feel about children, were you going to say? I'm past all that,' he told her flatly. 'Haven't felt anything in a long time. You've no cause to worry. I won't throw a wobbly.'

'You haven't seen Tom Cavanagh, your oncologist, since you left, have you?' she said, voicing a concern that she'd had all the time he'd been absent.

'No, I haven't. But I've been seeing someone where I've been living and am still clear of the cancer.'

'Thank goodness for that,' she breathed, and thought of the time when Mr. Cavanagh's secretary had phoned to say that Steve needed to make an appointment for a check-up and she'd had to tell her that she didn't know where he was.

'So what's going on in the practice?' he asked, when he'd finished eating.

'You'll find that nothing has changed much. Most of the staff you'll know from before. I still take the ante-natal clinic and the practice nurses the diabetic and blood-pressure clinics.'

'Who did Colin take on to replace me?'

'No one at first, as we were expecting you back,' she told him, trying to keep her voice steady. 'When that didn't happen, he employed locums, but in the end it became just the two of us. We both felt it was easier that way.'

'Why was that?'

'Because Colin never found anyone as good as you.'

'But with me missing, there would have been extra work.'

'Yes, there was—a lot of it. It was fortunate that I had nothing else to occupy me.'

He didn't take her up on that. He'd got the message. He'd left her private life empty and her working life was all she'd had. It would be a miracle if Sallie ever looked at him again.

When they'd finished discussing practice matters, Steve got to his feet. It was late and he wanted to get the embarrassment of going into the guest room over.

'I think I'll turn in,' he said. 'What time do you get up in the mornings?'

'Sixish. Liam wakes up around about then and his first thought is food.'

He smiled. 'Of course. Goodnight, then, Sal…and thanks for letting me come back into your life. I'm not asking for anything other than the chance to do a good job in the practice and, if I can, make amends for what I did to you.' And before she could reply to that he went into the spare room and closed the door.

She was standing rooted to the spot when it opened again and he appeared dressed in just boxer shorts, on his way to the bathroom.

'What?' he asked.

'Nothing,' she whispered, having forgotten that these kind of intimacies would be unavoidable living under the same roof. 'I'm just going to check on Liam.'

'Am I allowed to come, too?'

'Er, yes, of course. After all, he is your niece's child. You have more claim on him than I have.'

As they stood side by side, looking down at the golden-haired occupant of the cot, Sallie was so aware of Steve's semi-nakedness that she thought he must surely pick up on it, but he turned away and said wryly, 'Life is so simple at this age, isn't it? As long as his basic needs are catered for, the little one hasn't a care in the world.'

With that he went to where he'd been going in the first place, and as Sallie heard him switch on the shower she went into the sitting room and collapsed onto the sofa.

She wasn't expecting it to be easy in the weeks to come. Yet it had seemed as natural as breathing to make the sandwich when she'd discovered that Steve hadn't eaten since midday.

She could hear the shower running and thought that showering together had been as natural as breathing too…once.

Raising herself slowly off the cushions she eased herself into an upright position and gazed down thoughtfully at the wedding ring on her finger. She hadn't taken it off, never would, even if they never got back together again.

Steve had taken one step in the right direction. He

was back in the home they'd shared together, but that wasn't going to heal the hurt he had caused. He had a long way to go before that was going to happen.

When Steve had finished showering there was no sign of Sallie and when he looked across at the main bedroom he saw that it was his turn to be faced with a closed door.

'Goodnight, Sal,' he said in a low voice, but there was no reply as she lay with Liam in his cot beside her.

As he turned away he thought wryly that it would seem that his return had been something of a damp squib, and he wondered if she saw it as just a temporary thing. That she saw him as nothing more than a lodger now. She'd said that she'd got used to living alone. That a person could get used to anything in time, and he was to blame for that.

As he lay sleepless Steve heard the clock of the village church strike in the silence of the country night. He was back where he belonged, he thought thankfully. He'd dreamt of this place all the time he'd been away, and at the centre of his dreams had always been Sallie and the children he hadn't been able to give her.

But now the only thing that mattered was that he make amends for the senseless thing he'd done in walking out on her. She was cool and distant, wary of him. Somehow he had to prove to her that it hadn't been because he'd loved her any less that he'd gone away.

When he appeared in the kitchen the next morning Sallie was feeding Liam and the baby's blue gaze rested on him briefly before it returned to where the food was coming from.

'He's a beautiful child,' he said. 'I don't know how Melanie could leave him for such a long time. If he was mine, I wouldn't want to let him out of my sight.'

'She had her reasons,' Sallie told him levelly. 'She's young, ambitious, has always wanted to be a dancer, and as a single parent she needs the money.'

'And you just happened to be around to look after the baby,' he said dryly. 'I would have helped out with the finances if she'd asked me.'

'Maybe, but her needs were immediate. She required someone who was there already, and as I was the only one around she turned to me. I wanted to help in any case and the thought of having this little cherub for six months was something I couldn't have refused.'

The baby's cereal bowl was empty and as she turned to place it on the worktop Steve picked up a baby wipe and cleaned Liam's face.

'I need to get dressed,' she told him, without commenting on the speed with which he was getting involved in baby care. 'Will you keep an eye on Liam?'

She knew he wouldn't say no to that, and when the answer came it was, 'Yes, of course.'

When she reappeared, dressed in a navy skirt and jacket with a white silk shirt, Steve was doing what she'd known he would be, cuddling the baby.

He looked up and said without explanation, 'Philip Gresty. What's the situation with him? I saw Anna at the garage when I came over that day and she told me he's got motor neurone disease.'

'There isn't much to tell. We both know that it is very debilitating and so does he. Philip has been Colin's patient so now he will be yours.'

"I should have been there for him,' he said regretfully, gazing back down at Liam.

'Well, you're here now,' she said briskly. 'But, time is passing. Hannah will take over here when she arrives. She should be here any moment.'

'What did she say when she heard I was coming back into the practice.'

'She was pleased to hear it. Hannah always doted on you.'

'Until I blotted my copybook.'

Sallie could have taken him up on that but their affairs were too important to be discussed in the few seconds before they went down to the surgery. Instead, she said, 'There's nothing to stop you from going down. I can't budge until Hannah appears. I suggest that we do the house calls together after the surgeries. The countryside hasn't changed much since you've been gone, but some of the people have.'

'Sure. Whatever you say,' he said easily, and made for the stairs.

He was too docile, she thought when he'd gone The drive and dynamism that had been so much a part of the man she loved had been damped down. Admittedly, it was of his own doing, but he'd had his reasons and though he'd broken her heart, she'd understood his despair.

She could hear Hannah's voice down below. Soon another day at the village practice would begin but there would be one big difference. There would be two Dr Beaumonts treating the sick, instead of one, and she couldn't help but be happy about that.

As Steve called in the last patient before he was due to start house calls, he was relieved that his first surgery was nearly over.

The patients he'd treated had been varied in their acceptance of him. Most of them knew him. Remembered him from before. Some had been curious, others hesitant when they'd seen a different face behind the senior partner's desk. but in the main they'd been too concerned with their health problems to ponder too deeply on the new arrangement.

One old farmer who'd come to see him about his lumbago did have a comment to make to those in the waiting room. 'I remember Steve Beaumont from when he was here before,' he announced, 'and he's a damn good doctor. Not one of those who won't come out at night, or is reaching for a prescription pad before you've had time to tell him what ails you, *and* his private life is his own business.'

But Steve hadn't heard the vote of confidence, and now he was being forced to sit and listen to what Maisie Milnthrop had to say, and *she* wasn't ready to pat him on the back by any stretch of the imagination.

Big of body and big of voice, the widowed octogenarian plonked herself down on the other side of his desk and said accusingly, 'So you're back.'

'Yes, that's right, Mrs Milnthrop,' he said levelly, bracing himself for what was coming next.

'Another woman, was it?'

'No, it was not. I left the village for health reasons.'

'Ah, picked something up, had you? I hope you didn't give it to that lovely wife of yours before you went, and it's to be hoped you've got yourself sorted if you're coming back here.'

He was angered by her attitude at first but then found himself wanting to laugh. The thought of being diseased and a person to be avoided was comical, but he wasn't going to rise to the bait and said, without raising his voice, 'You're free to think what you will of me, Mrs Milnthrop. For my part, I'm here to treat the sick, so is there anything I can do for you?'

'Er no, there isn't,' she told him with rising colour, and got to her feet. 'You're a cool customer, I'll grant you that.'

As she stomped out Steve shook his head. What would she have to say if she knew the real reason why he'd left the village? Would he go up in her estimation, or down?

Doing the house calls with Sallie also had its fraught moments but in a different way. He'd phoned Anna Gresty to say that he was coming to see Philip, and when she'd told her husband he'd been delighted.

Talking wasn't that easy for him, but when Steve arrived Philip managed to say, 'I've missed you, lad. I know you wouldn't have gone away without a good reason because of the way you felt about Sallie, but, whatever it was for, it's good to have you back.'

Steve nodded. 'It's good to be back,' he told his friend, and felt like weeping. The robust farmer was now a sick man. He was having difficulty swallowing and was suffering from muscle weakness that prevented him from walking properly and holding onto anything. His was already an existence of slow deterioration and when Anna told him how Philip never complained, Steve thought that his own problems had been as nothing compared to his friend's.

Philip hadn't had anywhere to run when *he'd* been struck down with a dreadful illness. His own cancer had been cured, but he hadn't been able to put it behind him because of the constant dread of infertility, and he'd gone off to suffer in solitude, instead of facing it with Sallie beside him.

'What about physiotherapy?' he asked, when he'd finished examining the sick man. 'Has Colin ever suggested it?'

'He was going to organise it,' Anna said, 'but the move came so suddenly it never got sorted.'

'Right. It's going to be sorted now,' Steve said briskly. 'I'll set it up as soon as I get back to the surgery. It won't be a cure, Philip, but it will help your movements and swallowing problems.'

'I'm beginning to feel better already,' Philip said, and Steve took his hand in his. 'Send for me if you need me,' he told Anna, 'and I shall be visiting regularly without being asked in any case. And now I'd better go and see what Sallie is up to.'

Sallie had wanted Steve to see Philip on his own not only because the farmer was his patient, he was also his dear friend. As he'd entered the farmhouse she'd gone to buy some of the farm produce that the Grestys' daughter was in charge of in her mother's absence.

As they drove back to the practice after completing the home visits Steve said, 'Maisie Milnthrop came in to see me during surgery.'

'That's strange. She usually asks to see me.'

'It wasn't a consultation. She'd come to give me the length of her tongue.'

'What for?'

'Leaving you, of course. She thought I'd gone off with someone else. When I told her she was mistaken, that it had been for health reasons, she still couldn't give me the benefit of the doubt and jumped to the conclusion that I'd picked up a nasty infection somewhere.'

'That sounds like Maisie,' she said wryly. 'What did you say to her?'

'I told her that she was free to think what she liked about me, but that I was there to treat the sick and was there anything I could do for her.'

'And what then?'

'She went, having said her piece. 'It wasn't pleasant, having my morals suspect. There's only one woman for me.'

'So you didn't feel the need while you were away all that time?'

He glanced at her sharply and Sallie couldn't believe they were having this conversation in cold blood.

'Oh, yes, I felt the need all right, but I do have some self-control.' He held her gaze. 'And as I've just said, there's only one woman for me.'

'And that being so…you left me.'

'I was a mess, Sal. You were better off without me.'

'I would have liked to be the judge of that.'

He sighed. 'Yes, I know, and having seen Philip this morning I realise that what happened to me doesn't compare with what life has done to him. I wanted to weep when I saw him.'

'At least you're here for him now,' she said in a gentler tone.

'Is that how you see *us,* Sal? Better late than never?'

'Ask me in six months' time. I need some breathing space.'

The big limestone house that combined the surgery and their apartment was coming into view and he said, 'In spite of Maisie's interference and my concerns for Philip, it's great to be back where I belong.'

'Yes,' she agreed. 'I think that everyone at the surgery was glad to see you, and all the village folk remember you as a "damn good doctor," which, I was told, was how one of the farmers described you earlier.'

There was no mention of just how glad *she* was to see him back, he noticed, and knew he had no right to expect that she should be.

* * *

When Sallie climbed the stairs at the end of the late surgery, Hannah was about to come down.

'Steve's just put the kettle on,' she said, 'and Liam is getting a cuddle.'

'Has Liam been good?' Sallie questioned.

'Yes. He always is. I've just brought him back from the park. The only time he complains is when he's hungry,' she said with a smile.

'Don't I know it!' Sallie said laughingly.

'It'll have been a strange day, no doubt,' her house-keeper-cum-nanny said, lowering her voice. 'Himself being back.'

'Yes, it has,' Sallie agreed. She couldn't remember a stranger one and wondered if Steve was thinking the same thing. At least she'd been in her natural habitat, while for him it must have been a mixture of many things.

He'd made a pot of tea and as they sat at the kitchen table, drinking the steaming brew, he said, 'So who's turn is it to cook tonight? Shall I do it?'

Sallie hesitated. It was what they'd agreed, but it had been a tiring day and outside the sun was still high in the sky. 'Why don't we have a stroll down to the shops and pick up fish and chips on the way back?' she suggested. 'You remember The Happy Fryer, well, it's still there, with Doreen and George in charge.'

He was smiling. Not the grimace that he'd been passing off as a smile so far, but the quirky grin that she remembered so well from the days when there hadn't been a cloud in their sky.

'Bags I push the pram,' he said, but instead of flashing him an answering smile she frowned.

'What? Why the long face?' he questioned.

'Liam is going to be with us for another five months. It will be a wrench for me when Melanie takes over and it will be the same for you if you get too attached to him.'

'Yes. I know,' he said levelly. 'But I've already told you that I've accepted that I'm not going to father any children. I'm over it, Sal. It took me long enough, I know, but you don't need to think that every time I'm near Liam I'm going to go into depression, because I'm not. Look at the bright side. I'm a great-uncle.'

'All right,' she conceded. 'So let's go, shall we?'

As they walked along the main street of the village, with Steve pushing the pram, Sallie decided to ask the question that had been in her mind since he'd come back. 'Would you have returned if it hadn't been for Colin wanting you back in the practice?' Her tone was casual, but she held her breath as she waited for his reply.

'Yes,' he said, observing her warily. 'I've been on the brink many times, but dreaded making a fool of myself. Colin's suggestion was heaven-sent. After what I'd done to you I expected you to send me packing the moment you saw me.'

'I accepted you back because of the practice. It was a case of working with a stranger or an estranged husband.'

'And you saw me as the lesser of two evils?'

'Mmm. Possibly.'

She sounded totally disinterested and his heart sank,

but as a warm sun shone down on them and friends and acquaintances stopped to have a peep at the baby and shake hands with him, he put the uncertainties of the future to the back of his mind.

When they'd eaten the fish and chips and Sallie had bathed and fed Liam and settled him down for the night, Steve disappeared into the spare room.

He needed time to unwind, he told himself. How could he have let the opportunity pass to tell Sallie that she was the reason he'd come back? That there was no other. That he'd ached to see her again so much there had been times when he'd actually set off to drive back to the place where he'd left his reason for living, but each time his stupid pride had made him turn back.

Leaving her was the cruellest, most irrational thing he'd ever done, and he'd told himself a thousand times that he deserved the misery it had brought him. And that was how it had been until one day an acquaintance had told him that Colin Carstairs had been trying to get in touch with him and he'd gone cold with dread.

There had to be something wrong with Sallie, he'd thought. Colin wouldn't be looking for him otherwise, and even as he'd thought it he'd been pointing the car towards Cheshire. It had never occurred to him that it might be connected with the practice and when he'd discovered that it had been, he'd grasped the chance to be near her with both hands.

That had sorted out his working life. When it came to his marriage it was another matter. He might be back under his own roof, but he wasn't back in his own bed, or likely to be in the near future, and yet he'd had a chance to do something about it as they'd walked through the village. But because he was afraid to take any chances with the frail bond that was forming between them, he'd let Sallie think that he'd come back just for the job.

As he gazed sombrely out of the window he saw that the garden at the back of the surgery was full of weeds. In that other life he had grown vegetables there, and as he observed the unkempt plot he was glad in a strange sort of way. Tidying it up would give him something to do in the evenings instead of being in Sallie's space. On impulse he changed into a pair of old jeans and went down there.

He stayed out until the sun went down and as he put the spade away and turned to go back inside she was there behind him, and he almost knocked her over. He reached out to steady her and as his hand gripped her bare arm she became still in his grasp.

It was the first time they'd touched in three years and he had to be holding her with a grimy paw, he thought miserably, and released his grip.

'Sorry about that,' he said flatly. 'I didn't know you were there.'

She smiled and, trying to keep her voice steady, asked, 'Are you ready for a coffee?'

Still shaken by the contact, he nodded. 'Yes, please. I'll be up as soon as I've changed my shoes and got cleaned up.'

There was silence as they sat in the sitting room with their coffee-cups a few minutes later and Steve wondered if that brief unromantic moment had affected Sallie as much as it had him.

It appeared not, as she looked up suddenly and, breaking into the silence, said, 'Laundry?'

'What?'

'I'm going to put the washing-machine on. Can I have your laundry?'

'Er…yes,' he said woodenly. 'I'll go and get it.' So much for imagining that she'd been as aware of him as he'd been of her. But, then, he was forgetting his place.

Nothing had been said about him being back in the apartment for good. Sallie might be expecting it to be a temporary thing, for all he knew.

When he'd finished his coffee and produced the washing that she'd asked for, he said, 'I'm off to bed, Sal. It's been a long day, stepping into Colin's shoes in the practice that I used to know so well and renewing my acquaintance with the villagers.' He didn't think it wise to mention that the most stressful part had been being so close to her physically but so far away mentally.

He paused outside the door of the spare room. 'Shall I get breakfast in the morning?'

She shrugged. 'Whichever of us is up first can get it started. I'm usually on the go about six.'

He nodded and, feeling that she saw him more as an encumbrance than someone to assist, told her, 'Fine. We'll take it as it comes, then.'

She'd watched him digging from the window and

been stunned. Was there no end to this strange day? She'd thought. Steve hadn't been back five minutes and he was attacking the wilderness down below. Maybe he'd had enough of the chill she was giving off and, momentarily repentant, she'd gone down to ask if he would like a drink.

When he'd grabbed her arm she'd wished she'd stayed inside. Touching wasn't in the deal as far as she was concerned. Yet when he'd apologised she'd felt like weeping, as he'd merely been trying to stop her from falling.

CHAPTER THREE

THE feeling of being an encumbrance was still there when Steve heard the baby crying in the middle of the night. It wasn't his normal lusty howl. It was a fretful cry and his first instinct was to leap out of bed and go to Liam, but would Sallie want him interfering?

He groaned. If it had been the old days, he would have already been there, not across the hall. At that moment the door flew open and Sallie was there, with Liam in her arms.

'Steve! Are you awake?' she cried. 'Liam has just brought up his feed. He's been sick all over the cot, himself and me.'

He was beside her in a flash, taking the fretful infant from her and cradling him to his chest. 'He feels as if he has a slight temperature, but that will probably disappear once his tummy settles down,' he told her.

She looked at Liam anxiously, 'Do you think he's sickening for something?'

'Maybe. We'll have to keep an eye on him. He's calm enough now and ready to go back to sleep, but first he needs changing. Find me some clean clothes and I'll wash and change him while you attend to yourself. Once you're out of the shower you can hold him while I strip the bedding off the cot.'

Steve was sitting by the bed, gently rocking the baby in his arms, when Sallie came out of the shower with a towelling robe fastened tightly around her and she felt tears prick. If he was like this with someone else's child, how would he have been with their own? she thought. And almost as if he'd read her mind, he looked up but didn't comment.

She looked scrubbed and clean, he was thinking, but why had she got the robe fastened so tightly? Was it because she was aware of the countless times he'd held what was beneath it?

'I'm so thankful that you were here,' she told him as she looked down at the now sleeping child. 'Those are the kind of moments when a helping hand makes all the difference.'

'It's nice to know that you haven't written me off entirely,' he said with a quirky smile, and saw her expression change.

'I was the one who was written off, Steve,' she said quietly. 'I adored you, loved you more than life itself. When you went, you took away my reason for living. For months, years I went through the motions, attending my patients and then coming home to this place where every inch of it reminded me of you.'

'I knew how much you were hurting, but so was I. Each day it became clearer that having only me wasn't enough for you. You couldn't just be grateful that Tom Cavanagh had made you well again. You had to have the full package, and when it wasn't available you gave up on us.'

Still holding Liam close, he got to his feet. 'Don't you think I know that? It's what I've had to live with for the past three years.' He held the baby out to her. 'Here, take Liam while I change the cot.'

When that was done he said, 'You know where I am if you need me again.' And immediately thought it had been a tactless thing to say when there had been such a long time when she hadn't had the slightest idea where he was. 'So goodnight. I'll see you both in the morning, and, Sallie, if I said I was sorry a thousand times, it wouldn't be enough to cover my regrets. My only excuse is that I was in total despair and couldn't face your kindness any more.'

As the door closed behind him she groaned. Every word of what she'd said had been true, but she'd missed out one thing. She hadn't told him that under her pillow was a shirt that he'd worn the day before he'd left. There'd been the smell of him on it, and ever since she'd held it while she slept. It was fortunate that he had left her to change her own bed or he might have seen it, and what would he have made of that?

As she emptied the washing-machine and filled it again with the soiled linen and nightwear, she was thinking that the difference in their characters had been what had attracted them to each other in the beginning, and in the end it was what had driven them apart.

In the traumatic summer of three years ago he had soon recovered physically from the operation, but mentally there had been scars that were not healing. His moods had alternated from brisk normality to being totally unapproachable. Loving him as she did, Sallie had understood, but had still felt bound to remind him that Tom Cavanagh had said there was no reason why he shouldn't father children. That his other testicle was perfectly healthy.

But as time had gone by and no babies had come along, with Sallie menstruating on the dot and Steve always as prickly as a hedgehog, she had begun to feel the strain. It had all come to a head on a dark winter's day when he'd said that if she'd agreed to them trying for a family when he'd first suggested it, they might have had a child by then.

'How dare you switch the blame onto me?' she'd cried. 'There's nothing to say I would have become pregnant if I'd done as you asked. No one is to blame, and just in case you're so wrapped up in your own self-pity that you can't think of anything else, there are lots of couples in our situation.'

'I was merely making a comment,' he'd said tightly. 'We both know who's to blame, me, because I no longer have the full equipment. You'd be better off without me. So I'll do you a favour.' And as she'd watched aghast he'd slammed into the bedroom, packed a case, grabbed his car keys and had been behind the wheel of his car before she'd gathered her wits.

She'd run out to try and reason with him but it had been no use and even as she'd pleaded with him, he had driven away into the night and out of her life.

* * *

When Sallie woke up the next morning after Liam's stomach upset she was aware of a shadow blotting out the light, and when she raised herself drowsily onto one elbow she saw that Steve was standing beside Liam's cot, looking down at him.

'What's wrong?' she asked, relieved that the shirt was nowhere on view.

'Nothing,' he replied in a low voice. 'I was just checking on Liam. He's still asleep and looks fine. I knocked on the door and when you didn't answer I thought you might have overslept after his little upset.'

She lay back on the pillows and looked up at him, with the events of the middle of the night crystal clear in her mind. It had been the old Steve who had helped her with Liam, brisk, businesslike and caring. Yet no sooner had she thanked him than she'd given him an angry version of her side of the break-up, without any reference to the misery he had endured during those long childless months after the operation. And now he was reduced to knocking on her bedroom door.

She wasn't to know that Liam wasn't the only one he'd been looking at. He had also been observing his wife, her cheeks flushed with sleep, hair splayed out across the pillow, the globes of her breasts rising and falling inside a thin cotton nightdress. He had told himself that he must have been out of his mind to have left her. But he'd been so full of hurt and anger because he'd been unable to give her a child that there had been no reason in him.

'Take your time,' he told her. 'It's only a quarter to six. I've made some tea. Do you want a cup?'

'Yes, please, but, Steve, before you go, thanks for sorting out the mess that Liam and I were in.'

He flinched. If only Sal could hear herself, he was thinking. It was as if she was talking to a stranger. But, then, maybe that was what she saw him as now. He bent and perched on the side of the bed and she inched away.

'You don't need to worry,' he told her. 'I'm not going to come on to you while things are how they are between us. If ever that happens again, it will be because you tell me you want me to.'

He was getting to his feet again and before she could reply he went into the kitchen and came back seconds later with the mug of tea. At that moment Liam awoke and lay smiling up at him.

'You do well to smile, young man,' he told him gently. 'Who was it that had us up and about when all decent folk should be asleep?' He lifted him out of the cot and held him close. 'You don't care, do you? All you are bothered about is a dry bottom and a full stomach.'

Liam's bottom lip was beginning to droop. He was about to start grizzling and they both knew why. The stomach in question was empty after the night's events.

'Shall I change him while you see to his breakfast?' Steve questioned.

She nodded. 'Yes, and you don't need to keep asking if it's all right. I'm grateful for your help.'

He smiled. 'Having Liam around is a bonus. The last

thing I expected was the two of us being involved in this sort of thing when I came back. Is he all right for clothes?'

'Those that Melanie left *are* getting a bit small,' she told him.

'So why don't we go shopping at the weekend?'

It was Sallie's birthday the following week and he knew he was going to have to tread carefully. Maybe if they went into the town together, he might see something to match up with what he'd brought with him.

She hadn't said yes to his suggestion of going shopping for Liam, but neither had she said no, so he would bide his time. If there was one thing his lonely exile had taught him, it was patience.

His first patient on that second day was Jack Leminson, the builder who did most of the repairs in the village and rarely had cause to step over the threshold of the surgery. But today it was a different matter. He was pale and drawn and when asked what the problem was said, 'I've got the most awful pain in my loin, Doctor. My mates at the pub have been telling me it'll be a kidney stone, but where would that have come from, and if it is, how do I get rid of it?'

'So why come to me if you've already been told what's wrong with you?' Steve said dryly.

Jack managed a weak smile. 'They were only guessing.'

'They might have been right, but I prefer to have some evidence before we start making guesses. If you'd like to go to the nurses' room, they'll give you a container for a urine sample and once that's sorted we'll send it off for analysis.'

When the patient returned, he confirmed to Steve that he'd had trouble passing urine.

'So, what's wrong with me?'

'There are signs that it *is* a kidney stone, Jack, but it could also be an infection.'

'But why? I've never had anything wrong with my kidneys.'

'Maybe not, but kidney stones can be caused by extreme dehydration. Have you been perspiring a lot lately? Not drinking enough perhaps?'

'Hmm.' Jack thought for a moment! 'I've been working near a boiler house in a factory and it's been roasting. I've been like a grease spot.'

Steve nodded. 'I'm going to refer you to hospital for X-rays and you may need specialist treatment. In the meantime I'm going to give you some painkillers. Go home to bed, take the tablets as prescribed, and get plenty of liquids down you.'

'It's the pain I want to see the end of as much as the stone,' Jack said, wincing as another spasm gripped him. 'Those at home won't believe it when they see me in bed. I've never had a day off work in my life.'

'So you've earned one,' Steve told him. 'Go and make the most of it. By the way, how's business.'

Jack smiled. 'Not bad, not bad at all. I've been doing mostly new properties of late. The factory job was a one-off. And speaking of new properties, would you happen to know anybody who'd be interested in buying a piece of land with planning permission to build a detached house on it?'

'Er…I might. Who does it belong to?'

'Me. It was my father's and he never did anything with it.'

"Where is it?'

'On Bluebell Lane by the riverbank.'

At that moment Steve knew he didn't want Sallie and himself to live in the apartment for any longer than they had to. It might be convenient, being above the surgery, but the place that Jack was talking about was only a couple of minutes' walk away. Yet he would be taking a huge risk if he bought the land and had a dream house built on it. Would she see it as a bribe, a peace offering or the fresh start that they both needed?

'I could be interested,' he told the builder, and for a moment Jack forgot the pain.

'Yeah?' he said in surprise. 'It's a gem of a spot. Have a walk down there and see for yourself. I could build you something really special on it.' As another stab of pain reminded him of why he was there he added, 'But I'll have to go home to bed. Keen as I am to make a living, I'm in no state at the moment.'

'There's no rush,' Steve told him. 'I'll go and have a look at it and get back to you. Is there a for-sale sign on the land?'

'Yes. You can't miss it.'

'Fine. So don't sell it to anyone else until I've viewed it.'

'I won't. I promise.'

The thought of building a new home hadn't occurred to him until the builder had asked if he knew anyone who wanted to buy a plot of land, and immediately he'd seen the merits of the idea. What Sallie would think about it he didn't know, but the more *he* thought about it, the more it appealed to him.

He'd stayed in some very average places over the last three years. He hadn't had to, but he'd been so low in spirits he hadn't bothered to look around and had taken what had been easily available. So the thought of a beautiful house by the river had caught his imagination and he supposed, if the worst came to the worst, he could live there by himself. But the whole idea was to build a house for Sallie where they could make up for the lost years, if she would let him.

They were going to do the house calls together again, and when he came out of his room after morning surgery Sallie said, 'There are a few visits to make and the nearest is to Henry Crabtree on Bluebell Lane.'

'Right,' he said casually, with the feeling that the fates were pulling his strings. 'I remember old Henry. What's the matter with him? I would have thought he'd be pushing up the daisies in the churchyard by now.'

'No such thing. He's elderly and becoming frail, but is a long way from being written off. He won the prize for the biggest marrow at the agricultural show last summer and this time he intends entering his tomatoes. The phone call from his daughter was to ask us to visit him as his face is puffy and discoloured.'

'Let's go,' he said.

Henry Crabtree's face was a mess, mainly across the bridge of the old man's nose and on his cheeks. There was a bright red area of raised skin that seemed to consist of blisters and crusted-looking pimples.

'When did the redness on your face first appear, Henry?' Sallie asked, after the two doctors had scrutinised the affected area.

'Yesterday,' he replied. 'I'd been feeling poorly for a couple of days with a bad head and vomiting and then this appeared. I wouldn't have bothered you, but my daughter, Caroline, said she was going to ring you on her way to work.'

'It is a good job she did,' Sallie said, and turned to Steve. 'Are you thinking the same as I am?'

'Erysipelas?'

'Yes. All the signs are there.' Turning to the old man, she said, 'Have you cut yourself, or had some other kind of open wound recently, Henry?'

The old man nodded. 'I cut me hand on a piece of glass that was hanging about in the shed. It wasn't a big cut, but it was deep. I thought nothing of it at the time.'

'That's probably the cause,' she said.

'What? You're saying that's why my face has puffed up?' Henry said in surprise.

'Yes. It has given you erysipelas. Are you allergic to penicillin at all?'

'No, not that I know of.'

Good. I'm going to put you on a penicillin-type medicine that should clear it up in a week or so. We'll drop the prescription off at the chemist's for you, and they will deliver it.'

'Thank you, Doctor,' Henry said gratefully. 'And if you don't mind my saying so, it's good to see you two together again. It was a sight for sore eyes when I saw you both coming up the path.'

Sallie smiled but didn't comment, and it seemed as if Steve hadn't heard. He was gazing intently out of the window. The building plot was next to Henry's cottage, and when they came out and Sallie saw the for-sale notice with planning permission she exclaimed, 'Somebody will soon snap this up! What a beautiful spot to build a house, with the river at the far end of the plot and fields at the front and side.' Her expression became dreamy. 'If it was mine I would build it from local stone, with all of it at ground level, and big windows and a green roof. And I'd have a lily pond and a gazebo in the garden.'

'Yes, well, there's nothing to stop you from wishing,' Steve said. 'This is one of the most beautiful spots in the village. Whoever ends up living here will be very fortunate.'

'I agree. I can't imagine anyone *not* wanting to live here,' she said as they walked back to the car.

You are going to have the opportunity, my beautiful Sallie, he thought. But when you discover who has bought the land, you might not be so keen. Because he *was* going to buy it. If he hadn't been certain before, he was now, having heard her describe the kind of house she would like.

Bluebell Lane was one of the prettiest parts of the village. Not far from the centre, yet quiet and secluded, with just a farm at the far end and Henry's cottage at the beginning. It was the perfect spot to build a dream home, but he would look a fool if Sallie refused to share it with him.

He hadn't forgotten her outburst of the night before. She'd made no secret of her hurt and he couldn't blame her. In that other life before he'd gone away, she would never have edged away from him as she had that morning when he'd perched on the side of the bed.

Buy the land, build the house, and see what develops, a voice inside him was saying. Your relationship with Sally has reached rock bottom. It can only improve.

When they arrived back at the surgery he went into his consulting room and, shutting the door behind him, rang Jack Leminson. His wife answered, and she said, 'He's followed your instructions, Dr Beaumont, and gone to bed, but if you'll hang on for a moment I'll tell him to pick up the bedside phone.'

'I want the land, Jack,' Steve told him without preamble, 'and I want you to build me a house on it, but on one condition—that my wife knows nothing about it until it is finished.'

'You have a deal,' the builder said. 'As soon as I'm back in circulation we can meet up and sort out the details. What sort of a house did you have in mind?'

'All at ground level, local stone, green roof, lily pond, gazebo…'

'Hey, steady on, Doc,' Jack said laughingly. 'The

only stone I'm interested in at the moment is the one that I'm trying to get rid of.'

'So do as I said,' Steve reminded him. 'Bed rest, lots of drinks and we'll see what the hospital says.'

It was another rash major decision he'd made, he was thinking as he went up to the apartment for a quick lunch with Sallie. But he felt deep down that this time it was going to be the right one, and if it turned out to be that it wasn't, that Sallie had had enough of him, then he would have to do his utmost to prove to her how much he wanted to make matters right between them again.

Living upstairs could be claustrophobic, and the thought of a spacious stone house on Bluebell Lane was the stuff that dreams were made of. But all his dreams centred around his wife, and if she could see this in the same way that he did, as a new beginning, a means of blotting out the last three years, he would rejoice.

She was already up there, chatting to Hannah and cuddling Liam.

'Hello, Steve,' the woman who was keeping their domestic ship afloat said cheerfully. 'There's soup warming and some sandwiches in the kitchen.'

'Thanks Hannah,' he said with a smile, and Sallie looked at him questioningly. He was his old self again for a moment, breezing into the kitchen with a decisive step. Something had pleased him and she wondered what it was.

Steve had been sombre at breakfast, which was not surprising after the happenings of the night before, and her reaction when he'd sat on the bed early that morning. But something must have gone right since.

Towards the end of the week she said casually, 'There are two things I need to ask you, Steve.'

'What are they?'

'Do you really want to be there when I buy a complete new wardrobe for Liam, and can we do one of the house calls together as I need your opinion?'

'Yes, in reply to both questions,' he said immediately. 'I can't remember when last I did any pleasure shopping... And who is the patient?'

'Elizabeth Drury. Do you remember her? Lizzie lives in Lilac Cottage on the main street. She recently had an operation and the wound isn't healing. It looks inflamed and the hospital has referred her to the local clinic to have it dressed daily.'

'And the clinic thinks it might be MRSA.'

'Hmm. I think it's unlikely, but I'm not happy about her being treated there. I feel that the hospital might be shirking its responsibility. But the trouble is, I've never seen MRSA. Have you?'

'Only once. A guy came to me with a very nasty sore on his back, and I mean nasty. It looked almost gangrenous. It turned out that he'd been in hospital for some weeks, had picked up the infection in a bed sore and it had shown itself a couple of days after he was discharged.

'Before I'd gathered my wits he'd developed pneumonia and, not willing to take any chances, I had him back in hospital smartish, and that was the diagnosis—

methicillin resistant staphylococcus aureus, MRSA. He recovered eventually but it was very serious for a while. So lead on to Mrs Drury and we'll see what's happening there.'

Lizzie Drury was not someone to make a fuss and when she saw the two doctors on her doorstep she laughed and said, 'Is this what they mean when they talk about a second opinion?'

Sallie smiled. 'Yes, it is. I've brought Steve along to have a look at your leg, Lizzie.'

'They've put an elastic stocking on and it feels a bit tight,' she told them, as she bent down to take it off.

Steve didn't touch the infected area but he scrutinised it carefully for some minutes and then, turning to Sallie, said, 'The skin is very thin on that part of the leg. That could be why the wound isn't healing as it should.' He asked Lizzie, 'Has anyone mentioned MRSA to you?'

She shook her head. 'No, but I have wondered.'

'I'd have a word with the clinic to see what they have to say,' he told Sallie. 'They will have been told what the problem is. If they are treating Mrs Drury for MRSA, you as her GP should be informed. Somehow I don't think it is the superbug. They would want to contain it where it was found, but I can understand your concern.

'The elastic stocking is all right as long as it doesn't affect circulation. They perhaps think the flesh will knit together better if it is held firmly in place, but for your own peace of mind ring the clinic.'

She nodded. 'Yes. I'll do that. Possibly you are right and the healing process is slow because the skin is so thin there. But I still don't like the idea of Lizzie's problem being the hospital's fault and yet they aren't seeing her in Outpatients.'

She lowered her voice. 'It's a wonder she isn't thinking of taking legal action.' She looked over at the old lady, who was now replacing the elastic stocking and smiled. 'Lizzie is a lovely woman. She told me that the hospital needs its money for more important things than paying out for a sore on her leg, which I thought was amazing in this world of claims and lawsuits for every little thing.'

As they drove away from Lilac Cottage, Steve suggested, 'Ring the clinic now and see what they have to say. I'll be interested to know.'

She did as he'd suggested and when the call was finished told him, 'There's been no mention of MRSA, according to the clinic nurse I spoke to. It would seem that the reason why Lizzie has been referred there is because of her age and the frailty of her skin. The hospital is admitting liability and don't want her having to travel into town every day for dressings. Even if she's picked up by ambulance, it would still be traumatic and very tiring for her, whereas the clinic is only at the other end of the village. But, needless to say, I'm going to keep my eye on that leg of hers.'

He nodded. 'Good thinking. And now, next on the agenda—clothes for Liam. And I intend to foot the bill. I wasn't there for Melanie when she needed me, so all the more reason for me to do my share now. So Saturday we go shopping. Right?'

'If that's OK for you. There are a few things I need to get for myself, too.'

'Likewise,' he agreed, and wondered just how his birthday gift to Sallie was going to be looked upon.

As Steve put Liam's foldaway pram into the boot of his car on Saturday morning Sallie stood watching with the baby in her arms. This was unreal, she was thinking. The two of them going shopping with this delightful child that they loved so much and who wasn't theirs even though it felt so right. She knew that Steve felt the same way she did. That it wasn't going to last for ever and they should cherish every moment he was with them.

He'd closed the car boot and was turning towards them and when he saw her expression he said, 'What? Why so serious? Is anything wrong?'

Ever since she'd appeared at breakfast-time with Liam in her arms and had found that he'd cooked for them and prepared the baby's bottle, she'd been able to sense that he was really looking forward to the day ahead and had told herself not to spoil it.

Yes, things were uncertain but she had to move on, and had vowed that she would try to stop harking back to the past. It was gone, and miraculously the future was slowly taking shape, though she still didn't want to be rushed.

She smiled and he thought how beautiful she was when she was happy.

'Nothing is wrong,' she told him. 'I was just thinking how much we both love Liam.'

Steve had an answering smile of his own. 'You bet. It will be a sad day for us when Melanie comes back to claim him, so let's make the most of it.' And they did.

In the children's department of a large store in the nearest town they bought day- and nightwear in various sizes and colours to allow for the baby's growth, and for the first time since Steve's return Sallie felt at ease with him as he stood beside her with Liam in his arms.

When they had finished he said, 'What about the shopping you need to do for yourself? Or shall we have lunch first? I see they have an attractive-looking bistro over there.'

'Yes, let's eat first, before Liam decides he's hungry. Then I'll do my shopping while you push him around the store, if that's all right.'

He laughed. 'Of course it's all right. I could do that for ever. Though it doesn't rate as high as feeding time, cuddling time and bathtime.'

Her glance was tender. Every time she saw Steve with Liam, the memory of the depth of his longing for a child, and the extent of his devastation in those awful months after he'd had cancer, came back.

When they met up again after she'd done her shopping he said, 'Liam is getting hungry. If you'd like to feed him I have a couple of things to get myself.'

'Sure,' she said easily. 'I'll be on the seat over there when you come back.'

He wanted to buy her a pair of amber earrings for her birthday. The jeweller's they had passed earlier had the style that he wanted. The purchase was soon made and within minutes he was back where he'd left her.

They headed back for home in the middle of the afternoon, with Liam asleep and Sallie and Steve lapsing into silence as they each thought their own thoughts. It wasn't long before the village came into view and it was time to unload their purchases and hope that the peace of the day would continue.

But when night-time came, nothing had changed. They went to their separate beds and Steve thought that a few hours of happiness weren't going to change that. The day when Sallie held out her arms to him and asked him to make love to her was going to be a long time coming.

While in the bedroom across the landing she was lying wide awake with his shirt in her arms and wishing that it could be him.

CHAPTER FOUR

STEVE had engaged an architect to draw up the plans and he had been told that Sallie's description of how *she* would want it to look must be followed to the letter, along with a couple of other things that she'd mentioned when she'd driven past and seen that the land had been sold.

'Someone has bought the land in Bluebell Lane,' she'd told him. 'I hope they will build something really beautiful on it.'

'Such as?'

'Well, like I said before, and with a garden room maybe, or a veranda, and a mooring stage by the river-bank, for canoeing or rowing.'

'Sounds fantastic,' he'd said. 'Maybe you should have gone into house design instead of health care.'

She'd smiled. 'Those are just my preferences. They wouldn't be everyone's, but it would be sacrilege if someone built something ultra-modern on it.'

'We'll have to see what develops, won't we?' he'd said as if only mildly interested, and the discussion had ended there.

* * *

The day before Steve signed the papers that would make the land in Bluebell Lane his, was Sallie's birthday and as it had approached he hadn't been sure how the gesture he wanted to make would be received.

In the years before their separation it had always been a very special day in his calendar, with a beautiful gift beside her breakfast plate on the morning, a special meal in the evening, sometimes followed by a show, and then to finish off the day they had made love, wrapped around with the special magic that they created for each other.

This time it would be very different. They had spent her last three birthdays apart and he knew that thought would be uppermost in Sallie's mind on the morning. There had been no gifts from him during that time and he was going to try to make amends.

She was in the kitchen, preparing Liam's breakfast, when he appeared, and while she was thus engaged he placed four packages beside her place at the dining table.

'It's a special day today,' he was telling the baby when she came in with baby rice in a bowl.

'Happy birthday, Sallie,' he said quietly, without moving. 'I hope that it will be happier than some you've had.'

Her glance was on the gift-wrapped packages. 'I would rather you hadn't bothered going through the motions,' she said stiffly. 'Especially when I think back to what my birthdays used to be like.'

She had put the bowl on the table and was looking down at his gifts without attempting to open them.

'I never forgot your birthday,' he said in the same

quiet tone. 'What you see there are my gifts to you for years one, two and three while we were apart, and the fourth is for today. Every time it came round I set off to bring your present and ended up turning back when I thought of what I'd done to you.'

At that moment Liam decided that breakfast was a long time coming and raised his voice, so Steve picked up the bowl and began to feed him. When it was empty he looked up. Sallie was weeping silently with the unopened packages still there in front of her.

He was by her side in a flash, desperate to comfort her, but she shook her head and told him, 'No, Steve. Just leave me alone. I was hoping that today would go by unnoticed like the others, and now that it hasn't I don't know whether to be happy or sad.'

'If you could be just a little bit happy, maybe,' he said gently.

And as the floodgates opened again she sobbed, 'I can try.'

When he came out of the spare room dressed for the day ahead, Sallie had just lifted Liam out of the bath and he was lying pink and perfect in a soft white towel in her arms.

'Liam is all yours,' she said. 'His clean clothes are out and there is some juice for him on the kitchen table. I'm going to get dressed.' Walking across to the table, she picked up the still unopened presents and carried them into the bedroom.

Steve gazed after her sombrely. He was getting just what he deserved, he thought, and hoped that if she ever did open the boxes inside the gift wrap she might realise the sequence of them. How after the first year of his absence the presents he'd bought had been follow-ups of the previous one.

In a flat velvet case was an amber necklace lying smooth and beautiful on black satin. It had been for the first of her birthdays that he'd missed. The second case held a matching bracelet, and in the third an elegant amber ring. To complete the set were the earrings that he'd bought when they'd gone shopping together. Whether any of them would ever see the light of day he didn't know, but at least Sallie had picked them up.

He'd chosen amber to match her beautiful hazel eyes and the dark gold of her hair, knowing instinctively that the pale cream of her skin would show them off per-fectly. Now all he could do was wait.

He hadn't booked a meal anywhere, deciding that it would be best to wait and see how his gifts were received, but he'd asked Hannah if she could come at short notice to take care of Liam if the opportunity was there. So far it looked as if he wasn't going to be trou-bling her.

Until Sallie came out of the bedroom with the ring on her finger and the earrings in her ears. She didn't meet his glance. Instead, she began sifting through the post that he'd just brought upstairs, and he got the message that she didn't want any comments. Yet it didn't stop his spirits from soaring.

In the lunch-hour he said, 'Hannah has said she'll come back this evening to take care of Liam if you would let me take you for a meal somewhere. Would you like that?'

Yes, she'd like it and, no, she wouldn't, Sallie thought. She was alone with him for hours on end when Liam had gone to bed, but in the apartment it was easy to keep at a distance. Beneath soft lights, with sweet music playing in the background, it wouldn't be so easy. Steve would be thinking that because she was wearing some of the beautiful jewellery he'd bought her, all was now right between them.

'I know what you're thinking,' he told her, 'and you're wrong. We don't get much time to relax with the practice and Liam to care for. A night out would be a pleasant change. You wouldn't be committing yourself to anything.'

'Yes, all right, then,' she agreed. 'Fix it up with Hannah.'

Concealing his elation, he said, 'Sure. No problem. Where would you like to eat. Town or village? I'm out of touch with wining and dining in these parts.'

'Village, I think. I don't want to be too far away from Liam. There's a big hotel about a mile away. I've never been there but have heard it highly recommended for dining out.'

'I'll try them now,' he said immediately, and by the time the lunch-hour was over Hannah had been asked to come back in the early evening and a table had been booked at the Kestrel Hotel.

As they drove there that night Sallie was aware of the strangeness of the occasion. She felt as if it was some sort of charade they were involved in, raking up old ashes that had been too long dead.

Yet she'd dressed with care in an outfit that Steve had always liked, a long cream silk dress, low cut, with a straight skirt that flared at the bottom, and over it a short black jacket. She'd hesitated about wearing any of the jewellery he'd given her, thinking that with the clothes *and* the jewellery he might forget that it was just a friendly night out, and she wasn't ready for anything else. So the amber collection was returned to the drawer.

He'd presented her with a corsage of apricot-coloured roses that would have blended beautifully with the jewellery if she'd worn it, and when he'd bent to pin it onto her jacket she'd said, 'When did you get this?'

He had raised his head slowly and as their glances had met he'd asked, 'Why? Does it matter?'

'It does if you had already bought it before I'd said I would dine with you.'

'For goodness' sake, Sal!' he'd exploded. 'I get your meaning. I'm not going to take you for granted. You need have no fears on that score. I take nothing for granted these days. But do feel free to remove the corsage if it would make you happier. I went to the florist in the village in the lunch-hour *after* you'd agreed to dine with me and asked them to make it up. I popped out to collect it while you were still seeing your patients. Does that satisfy you?'

'Yes. I'm sorry,' she'd told him, and had thought how

far away they were from how they used to be. And now, with the vibes of that little episode hanging over them, they were about to spend the whole evening together, and it was like being on a first date.

He reached across and took her hand. 'No, *I'm* sorry, Sal. All I want is for you to have a brighter birthday than those of recent years. So let's relax and enjoy ourselves and forget about all the side issues in our lives for tonight.'

They did that by enjoying the food and keeping the conversation light, not letting each other see how much they were aware of one another.

At eleven o'clock Steve said, 'I think we should go, Sallie. Hannah is a good soul and I don't think we should be keeping her up until all hours.'

She smiled across at him. 'I agree, and then there is a certain baby that we've been away from long enough.'

When he stopped the car in front of the surgery, she said, 'Thanks for a lovely evening, Steve…and for remembering my birthday.' She reached across and kissed him on the cheek and he became still. As she drew back into her seat he said, 'You do know that I never stopped loving you, Sal.' And waited for her response.

'Yes, I know,' she replied, and that was all. Nothing to cling to regarding how *she* felt about *him*.

The plans had been passed after weeks of waiting and now Jack was ready to start building. When Steve had asked him how long it would take, he said, 'If the weather keeps fine, about three months. That's if we don't get any hold-ups with materials and so on. We'll soon be into autumn so we need to get the shell finished before winter sets in.'

'You haven't forgotten that it is still a secret from my wife,' Steve reminded him. 'I want to present it to her when it's finished as a complete surprise.'

When Steve called to see Philip Gresty one afternoon the sick farmer said, 'I'm told that the land that was for sale on Bluebell Lane has been sold. Do we know who's bought it?'

Rather than tell a lie, Steve shrugged and said, 'No doubt everyone will soon find out.'

The physiotherapy was giving Philip some relief, and on that particular day he was in good spirits because his daughter was soon to be married.

'Who is the lucky man?' Steve asked.

'Dale Barraclough from Moorend Farm. I've said he can take over here when I'm gone, but because he's got an earring and has his hair down his back, Anna isn't so sure about him. I've told her as long as he can plough a straight furrow, he'll do for me.'

Harvesting time had come to the village. The farmers were gathering in their crops. Neat bales were appearing in the midst of fields of golden grain, and fruit was being plucked from trees laden with ripe apples and pears.

Some of the hardier folk went daily up onto the moors where the wild windberries were now ripe for picking to make tarts and preserves, and as the two doctors watched them plodding upwards to where the fruit grew close to the ground, they knew that the 'bad back' season was about to commence.

It was a painstaking task, gathering the berries one by one. It meant bending for hours on end, and there was always someone who overdid it at the thought of gorging on the succulent fruit of the moors.

On a Sunday morning in late September, Sallie, Steve and Liam joined the villagers inside the ancient church in a service of thanksgiving for the harvest that had been gathered in.

Anna Gresty always baked a huge cob in the shape of a sheaf of corn for the event and it was placed in a central position below the pulpit. Then the farmers appeared with gifts from whatever produce they had grown, and last but not least came the children, carrying their own small offerings of fruit and vegetables, which, like the farm produce, would be distributed to the needy after the service.

As the children paraded around the church with their gifts, Sallie glanced at Steve. He was holding Liam, looking down at him in his arms, and she wondered just how much he was hurting inside. Was he thinking that everyone had a child except them? Because Liam belonged to someone else.

He looked up, their eyes met and he shook his head as if to say, Stop worrying. It's sorted.

They had Liam's pram with them and after the service Sallie said, 'Let's take a walk down Bluebell Lane to see how that house is coming along.'

'Sure,' he said easily, knowing that the builders wouldn't be there, it being Sunday.

They were up to the roof now, but he already knew that as he made the opportunity to drive past each day now that he and Sallie weren't doing the house calls together.

It was all going to plan. The local stone, the big windows and the green-tiled roof, which he was hoping wouldn't give the game away. It didn't. When she saw it she said, 'Someone, somewhere has got the right idea.' He hoped she would still be of the same opinion when it was completed and he asked her to live there with him.

He had a call from Anna during the following week and went out to the farm straight away. He found Philip looking pale and exhausted. It appeared that at the time of Anna's call the muscles of his throat had not been functioning and she'd been afraid he was going to choke, which was one of the distressing features of the illness. But by the time he'd got there the problem had eased off.

The Grestys were envied by some of the village folk as everything they touched seemed to prosper. Only he and Sallie knew that Philip was not to be envied at all.

When he'd become Philip's GP again Anna had told him that the motor neurone disease had first manifested with muscle cramps, followed by weakness and involuntary movements of the legs. He had gone for extensive tests, including measurement of electrical activity in the muscles and a myelography, an X-ray of the spinal cord. In the end, after weeks of worry, had come the dreaded diagnosis.

And now Philip, who should have had many good years ahead of him, was having to take stock of what the future held and it was not good. Slow, painful deterioration was on the cards.

'Why us, Steve?' Anna said tearfully, just as he was about to go. 'We've always worked hard and minded our own business. Helped others when we could. And now Philip has got this terrible illness that affects only one or two people out of a hundred thousand each year.'

'I can understand how you feel,' he told her, 'but in Philip's case it's a genetic thing. I believe he had an uncle who had it.'

She stared at him aghast. 'Do you mean his Uncle Jim? I remember him being in a wheelchair, but he died before we were married, so I didn't know much about him. Is Philip sure about that? He's never mentioned it to me.'

Her face crumpled. 'And I know why. We have a daughter, haven't we? What about Janine? Is she likely to get it?'

'Not necessarily,' he reassured her gently. 'There is a fifty per cent chance she may have inherited the faulty gene, however. Anna, there is support available and I can refer you and Janine for genetic counseling, if you wish, to discuss your concerns and any tests available!'

"I don't know,' Anna said dismally. 'Maybe it's better not to know. What can we do if she's got it?'

'Why not let her decide? She's getting married soon, isn't she?'

'Yes, she is. This is a nightmare.'

'I know, but I'm here to support you,' he told her. 'Let

me know what you decide about genetic counselling, and remember this, Anna, they are both fortunate to have you. It makes all the difference when suffering from a serious illness to be able to rely on the love of those nearest to us. I know. I've been there and I walked away from it.' She looked at him in surprise. 'You have no idea how glad I am to be back where I belong.'

'What's wrong?' Philip asked when Anna came back from showing Steve out and he saw her stunned expression.

'Did you know that Stephen Beaumont left Sallie because he had a serious illness?'

'You're kidding!' he exclaimed weakly. 'Steve is as strong as a horse.'

'Was maybe.' And kissing him gently on the brow, she began to straighten his cushions.

'Did Colin know that Philip Gresty's illness is genetic?' Steve asked that evening as he fed Liam while Sallie was preparing their meal.

She looked up from chopping vegetables and observed him questioningly. 'Why? Is it?'

'Yes, it is,' he said sombrely. 'He told me the first time I saw him after I came back, but as Anna didn't know, and Colin hadn't discussed the chances of Janine getting it, I'm wondering if Philip has kept quiet about it to everyone except me, to prevent more anguish for his family.'

'Colin didn't always discuss his patients with me, or I mine with him,' she said, returning to what she'd been doing. 'And with regard to Philip, Colin might have thought that as he was a great friend of yours, it would upset me to talk about him.'

'And would it have done?'

She shook her head. 'No. Why should it? On the odd occasion I spoke to the Grestys while you were away, it was clear they knew nothing of our affairs.'

They do now, he thought, and could imagine the disbelief on Philip's face when Anna told him what he'd said. He hadn't been able to tell Maisie Milnthrop, but the Grestys were a different matter.

The six months of Sallie being in charge of Liam would soon be coming to an end and that same night Melanie rang to say that she'd fallen in love with an American and intended taking Liam back there once her contract was up.

It was Steve who answered the phone and he said immediately, 'Really? *I'm* known for making hasty decisions, but not when it comes to a child's future.' He sighed. 'Look, you're Liam's mother and can do what you want, but are you sure that's the right thing to do? To take him away from all he's ever known? Sally adores him, you know.'

He wasn't going to go into details about his own feelings for the baby. It was better left unsaid in the present climate. But he was angry at Melanie's attitude and she could tell.

'I would never do anything to harm my baby,' she said defensively. 'The guy I've met knows I've got a child and doesn't mind. He's in the show. Another dancer like me.'

'And what happens to Liam when you are both offered another contract?'

At that moment Sallie came into the room, carrying the child in question.

'Who's that?' she asked, taking note of his expression.

'My niece,' he said heavily and turned back to the phone. 'When are you coming to get him?'

'I don't know,' she said hesitantly. 'I'll ring again when I know what my plans are.'

'Yes, do that,' he agreed dryly, dreading what it would do to Sallie if Melanie did what she was thinking of doing.

'What was all that about?' Sallie asked, and when he told her she clutched the baby to her as if Melanie was going to appear at that moment. Yet what she had to say didn't fit in with that instinctive reaction.

'Melanie won't do anything to harm Liam,' she said gravely. 'She loves him, and after one bad relationship she won't risk another. But you were quite right to be concerned that she is doing the right thing. She'll ring again soon. You'll see…and, Steve, thanks for caring about us. Melanie, the baby and me.'

'You've got it in the wrong order,' he said lightly, his temporary annoyance having abated.

She didn't take him up on that, just passed Liam to him and said, 'Do you want to put him down for the night while I clear away after the meal?'

'Of course,' he said, looking down into their charge's unblinking blue gaze, 'That was your mummy on the phone, Liam. She wants to take you to live in America.'

'And we have no say in the matter,' Sallie reminded him, but he pretended he hadn't heard.

Melanie rang again the following night, as Sallie had said she would. It was Steve who picked up the phone again and if what she'd had to say the previous night had been surprising, this time it was even more so.

'I've thought about what you said, Uncle Steve,' she told him, 'and of course you're right. We've talked about it and agree that Liam needs a more settled life than Rick and I could offer him as dancers. So...could you find us somewhere to live in your village when our contracts are up? It's the perfect place for Liam to grow up and we'll look for employment locally.'

'Yes, of course,' he said immediately. 'Sallie will be delighted. She's just settling Liam for the night, I'll go and get her and you can tell her your plans yourself.'

He hadn't been wrong. Sallie was delighted. 'We'll be able to see Liam grow up,' she said happily, 'and as you are Melanie's only relative, you'll be able to keep an eye on her and the baby. As for the new man in her life, if he's willing to put his career on hold for their sakes, he must be genuinely devoted to her.'

She sighed. 'But it won't be easy to find them somewhere to live. It's rare that anything small and reasonable comes up for sale in the village, and even if it did, they won't have that kind of money.'

'Somewhere to rent would be the best thing,' he said thoughtfully, 'or rent-free, if such a thing exists.' He was thinking that he knew just the place, but it would depend on a couple of things How soon the house was ready for occupation and if Sallie wanted to move into it with him. If by some miracle she did, Melanie and Rick could have the apartment rent-free. He and Sallie owned it, so there would be no problem there.

They were both in high spirits for the rest of the evening, but beneath the lightheartedness Sallie was wondering just how much Steve really had accepted their childlessness. It had been upsetting enough during those fraught months after his operation when no pregnancy had been forthcoming, but he'd made it ten times worse by creating a three-year break in their lives.

Something had changed, though, in recent weeks. He might be wary of putting a foot wrong, but she sensed some sort of purpose in him. A kind of controlled excitement. Sometimes in the evenings he went out for short periods without explaining where he'd been, and there was no way she was going to ask. She knew that he visited Philip regularly, but didn't think it was to the Gresty farm that he went on those occasions.

The next morning, Steve went to visit Philip and found him lying on the sofa in the sitting room. Philip tried to raise himself to a sitting position when he saw Steve but had had to give up.

'How are you today?' he'd asked.

'Not good,' Philip said. 'Some days are worse than others.'

Steve nodded. 'So let's have a look at you to see what's been happening since I was here last. But before

I do that, have you spoken to Janine about the genetic side of your illness?'

'Yes,' he said sombrely. 'She's out giving a riding lesson at the moment, but is due back any time and wants a word with you.'

'How did she react when she knew that your uncle had the illness?'

Philip gave a grim smile. 'She'd already worked it out for herself. My daughter is no fool. She'd read motor neurone disease up in various medical books and knew the score.'

'So what about her being tested to see if she has the rogue gene?'

'That's what she wants to talk to you about. We know what she's decided, but she wants to tell you herself.'

At that moment Janine came striding into the sitting room, dressed in riding clothes and looking the picture of health.

'Can we have a word outside, Dr Beaumont?' she asked.

'Yes, of course,' he replied, and with a smile for the man on the sofa said, 'I'll be back shortly, Philip. Don't run away.'

'That will be the day,' he grunted, and waved them out of the room.

'Your father has told me that you are aware of the genetic implications of his illness,' Steve said once they were alone

'Yes,' she told him calmly. 'I've known from the beginning, but I've only just found out that his uncle had it. It would seem that you were the only person who knew that.'

'That is so, but *I* didn't know that and mentioned it to your mother. She was immediately very concerned on your behalf.'

'Yes, I know, and when she told me I wasn't exactly over the moon either. I've thought about it long and hard and have discussed it with the man I'm going to marry, and he and I are agreed that what we don't know about we are less likely to fret about.

'I wanted to call off the wedding. Didn't think it was fair to Dale to marry me with something of that sort hanging over me, but...' Her composure faltered for the first time and there was a wobble in her voice as she went on to say, 'He says if he doesn't marry me, he won't marry anybody. So that's what we've decided. We know the risk. Yet there are lots of people in Dad's family and no one else has been struck down with motor neurone disease so far.

'I might change my mind about all this when, or if, we want to start a family. I wouldn't want to bring a child into the world if I had the gene and might pass it on to my baby. But we're not bursting to become parents for a long while yet.'

'I can see the sense in your reasoning.' he told her. 'Out of those who do have the illness, it is only a small percentage who develop it from genetic sources. The trouble with motor neurone disease is that no one knows where it comes from. If they did, the medical profession might be able to do something about it. Yours will have been a difficult decision to make and I can tell that it hasn't been made lightly.'

When he went back into the sitting room Philip looked at him anxiously and Steve said reassuringly, 'Janine has told me what she's decided and I will respect her decision. She might want to change her mind at some time in the future and the opportunity to know for certain will still be there.

'And now what about you? I can see that your breathing isn't good. How's it been since I saw you last week?'

'Difficult,' Philip wheezed. 'I never go upstairs these days.'

'How about a stair lift?'

'I suppose we could get one fitted. Though I want to be as little trouble as I can for Anna.'

'Pressing a button to send you upstairs isn't going to cause her any problems.'

'All right, we'll see to it,' he promised. 'And by the way, I believe you told Anna that you were suffering from a serious illness when you left the village, yet you never said anything.'

'That was because I didn't want to talk about it. I had cancer.'

'Cancer? Oh, no!'

'Oh, yes, I'm afraid. I had to have one of my testicles removed. I've been clear ever since, but it seems as if the operation has made me infertile, and I was so desperate for a child I just couldn't cope. The guy who did the surgery said my other testicle was perfectly healthy, that I should be able to father children, and apparently it still is. But the chances of me ever making Sallie pregnant are doubtful.

'All our efforts to make a baby in the months after the surgery came to nothing and suddenly I snapped. Sallie was there for me every step of the way, but I just couldn't stand any more kindness. And there you have it.'

'And we never knew!'

'Nobody knew, except Sallie and Colin. I was so knotted up with hurt pride and frustration I wasn't fit to live with, and in the end I took myself off.'

'And you came back because of the vacancy in the practice?'

'Yes, in a way. I'd wanted to come back for a long time, but wasn't sure what sort of a reception I would get from Sallie. When Colin asked me to take over from him, it was the answer to my prayers—the chance to come back with some dignity, even though I didn't deserve it. When I look at you, and think of what I was like then, I could die of shame.'

'You shouldn't feel like that,' Philip said firmly. 'For a man who desperately wanted children, it must have been a nightmare.'

'It still is, but I'm not here asking for sympathy. I'm here to see you. Now, tell me exactly how you feel with regard to breathing, swallowing and mobility.'

CHAPTER FIVE

Driving back to the surgery, his conversation with Philip was uppermost in Steve's mind. Telling his friend about the past had been a reminder that Sallie was keeping her thoughts about it to herself for the most part. Except for her early morning outburst after Liam's gastric upset. It had been then that he'd told her he would never ever make love to her again unless she asked him to, and he'd meant it.

But it didn't stop the ache inside him when at the end of each day they went to their separate beds. One night he heard her sob in her sleep and when the sounds of distress came again he went and quietly opened the door of the main bedroom.

The curtains were drawn back and in the light of a full moon he could see the outline of Liam's cot and beside it the slender figure of his wife in the king-size bed. As he looked down at her his eyes widened. Deeply asleep, she was clutching an old shirt of his in her arms, and as he tried to take in what he was seeing hope was born.

He knew better than anyone that when one was

missing a person desperately to be able to hold onto something belonging to them brought a degree of comfort. In his case it had been a soft leather glove of Sallie's that he'd found in the glove box of the car.

When he'd known he was going to be seeing her in the flesh, he'd put it back where he'd found it, and there he intended it to stay as a reminder of the biggest mistake he'd ever made.

He knew instinctively that she would not want to come out of her dreams to find him standing over her while she was clutching his shirt. So he quietly went back to bed and for the first time since his return slept dreamlessly for the rest of the night.

At breakfast the next morning Sallie was her usual self and it was hard to imagine that he'd heard her sobbing in her sleep. He'd glanced through the open door of the bedroom as he'd made his way to the kitchen and there had been no sign of the shirt.

It was almost as if he'd dreamt the whole episode, but he knew he hadn't. He also knew it wouldn't be a good idea to mention it. If Sallie thought he was prowling around the bedroom while she was asleep, she wouldn't be happy about it. She might want a bolt on the door, and that really would be reducing their present situation to a sorry state of things.

Liam was old enough to sit in a high chair now and it was smiles all round from him as Sallie gave him his breakfast. As Steve was pouring himself a glass of juice, she said suddenly, 'I passed the house on Bluebell Lane yesterday. I couldn't see much of it from the road as it's set well back among the trees, but it was clear that the builders are making good progress.

'One of the workmen was coming off the site as I stopped to look and I asked him who had commissioned them to build the house. He said he didn't know, that only the boss, Jack Leminson, knew, and all he was saying was that it was for someone who had once lived in the area.'

'So you're no wiser.'

'No. I suppose I was being nosy, asking. But there is something about the place that seems to reach out to me.'

'Really? I wonder why,' he murmured.

As they waited for Melanie to come back from America, Sallie couldn't understand why Steve wasn't doing anything about finding the two dancers somewhere to live. She'd come up with a few suggestions of her own, but he always seemed to have a reason why they wouldn't be suitable and, being unaware of what was going on in the background, she didn't understand his lack of concern.

She hoped that he wasn't going to suggest they all live together for a time, as there just wasn't enough room. It would be chaotic. But knowing how fond he was of Liam he might see it as a way of staying near him, she thought.

With no such idea in mind, Steve was checking dates and schedules and trying to put his plans in place, but it seemed as if Melanie was going to be home before the house was finished, and they were going to have to start vetting any accommodation that was available.

To his relief, she phoned yet again with another change of plan, informing them that the show had been extended by two months and would it be too much to ask of them to care for Liam for a little while longer?

This time it was Sallie who answered the call and told Melanie, 'Of course we will. As a matter of fact, we haven't found you anywhere to live yet. We are working on it and the extra two months will give us more time to find something. But,' she cautioned, 'don't leave it any longer than that, Melanie. These are precious days in your baby's life and you're missing them.'

'Yes, I know, Sallie,' she said in subdued tones. 'I won't stay over here a moment longer than I have to. I'm only hanging on for the money.'

'So it means we have more time to find them accommodation,' Steve said when he heard what had been arranged. He looked relieved and she thought that she'd been mistaken in thinking he wasn't concerned.

The next day he waited until he was away from the surgery and then phoned Jack Leminson.

'When will you be able to give me a completion date?' he asked.

'Soon,' he was told in a cautious manner.

'How soon is soon, Jack?'

'You'll be in for Christmas. Is it still meant to be a surprise?'

'Yes, as far as I'm concerned.'

'Well, watch out when you come round here that old Henry Crabtree doesn't see you. He lives next door and wanders around the site, picking up any bits of wood lying around for his fire. He's very curious about who his new neighbours are going to be, and as the old guy is no fool you can bet your life he'll put two and two together if he gets a sight of you.'

'It's a wonder he hasn't seen me already, then.'

'He'd have said if he had. Henry likes to chat.'

For as long as anyone could remember, there had been a café on the main street of the village. It had been a clean but rather old-fashioned place that had served meals and snacks to villagers and also to the walkers who came and went through the beautiful Cheshire countryside.

At the end of summer the elderly couple who owned it had retired and moved into private accommodation, and there had been no activity there since, much to the disappointment of those who loved to explore the countryside all the year round.

As Christmas approached there were suddenly signs of life inside the empty café. Old fixtures and fittings were being ripped out and a new kitchen was being put in. The shopfront was being altered and new furniture being delivered.

It created much interest among local residents. Some were saying that they hoped it wasn't going to end up a glass and chrome establishment as that wouldn't fit in, and others felt that, whatever it turned out to be like, it would be an improvement on what had been there before.

When Steve saw that Jack's firm was involved in the

refurbishment he went round to Bluebell Lane to make sure that the work on his house wasn't coming to a halt because of the other job.

'No,' Jack told him. 'The gang at the café are extra men I've taken on. I know how keen you are to have your property finished, and it *will* be completed by Christmas at the latest. It's my eldest daughter, Cassandra, and her partner who've bought the café. They've put every penny they've got into it, taken out a hefty loan and are determined to make a success of it.'

'That shouldn't be hard,' Steve commented. 'There's no competition. Walkers with muddy boots won't want to lunch at the Kestrel, will they?'

The builder sighed. 'It's clear that you're not tuned into the grapevine. Someone has applied for planning permission to open a coffee-bar right opposite.

'Really! That's unfortunate.'

'Sure is,' Jack said. 'We'll just have to hope that the demands of the two don't overlap. The café will be open very soon, so it will have time to make its presence felt before anything happens regarding the coffee-bar.'

When he told Sallie about the café he said, 'So I suggest that we dine there sometimes to give the young couple some support.' She didn't agree or disagree, just asked where he'd got his information from, and as there was no way he was going to tell her that, in case she started putting two and two together, he skirted around the truth by telling her that it seemed to be general knowledge.

The activity continued and, finally, Cassie's Place was due to open the following Saturday. 'How about we eat at the new café on its first day of opening to help give it a boost?' suggested Steve. 'We can either take something with us for Liam, or order a baby portion for him.'

It hadn't been mentioned since he'd first told Sallie about it and he wondered if she'd remembered him suggesting that they should eat there sometimes. If she had, she didn't seem to be in any hurry to take him up on it and now she seemed only mildly interested as she said, 'Yes, I suppose we could. I know Cassandra Leminson from way back. She was a wild child.'

'Surely that isn't why you aren't keen on going?'

'Not necessarily.'

'Or could it be that you just don't want to go with *me*?'

'You're reading an awful lot into a moment's hesitation,' she said. 'Of course we'll go if that's what you want. If we don't support local traders, we won't have any shops or cafés.'

She wasn't going to tell him that she'd had to call someone into her consulting room to restrain the difficult teenager on one occasion after the girl had struck her.

It had happened after Steve had left and was all water under the bridge as far as she was concerned because Cassandra's hormones had been all over the place at the time. She'd generally been a very mixed-up teenager.

Sallie was pleased to hear that she was settling down and wished her and her partner success in their new venture, but it didn't stop her from wishing that it was someone more amenable that Steve was so keen for them to support.

For his part, Steve wondered if it was always going to be that way, that every time he suggested doing something together, it turned into an issue.

'Hello, Dr Beaumont,' Cassandra said awkwardly when she saw her. 'Thanks for supporting us on our opening day.'

Sallie looked around her and smiled. 'This is really something, Cassandra. You've transformed the place.'

She was thinking that the twenty-two-year-old had also transformed herself. The tarted-up, overweight adolescent had been replaced with a slimmer, toned-down version and it could have a lot to do with the toddler that the Leminson family were so devoted to.

The walls of the café had been painted in the palest of sunshine yellows, with views of the surrounding countryside hung upon them. The tables and chairs were of light golden wood with bright turquoise cloths, white china and sparkling cutlery, and beyond them, clearly on view was an immaculate kitchen.

'Thank you,' the young proprietress said, her colour rising, and turned to the young man beside her, who was wearing a chef's hat. 'Can I introduce my partner, Jonathan?'

When they'd shaken hands Cassandra's glance went to Liam, who was looking around him from the safety of Steve's arms, and she remarked, 'I didn't know that you had a baby.'

'He isn't ours,' Sallie explained. 'Liam belongs to my

husband's niece. We've are looking after him while she's working abroad.'

'Where would you like to sit?' Jonathan asked Steve.

'Wherever there's room for a high chair beside us,' Steve replied and they were shown to a table in the corner.

When they were seated Cassandra presented them with menus and before she left them to make their choices she turned to Sallie and said, 'I've been at catering college for the last two years and have had family responsibilities that have kept me busy, so this is an opportunity for me to say how sorry I am for being so difficult and abusive the last time I was at the surgery. I was a horror in those days, but being escorted from the surgery by the police and having to face up to my problems did me a world of good.'

'Yours were difficult teenage years,' Sallie told her. 'Some people sail through them, while for others they are not easy. It's been good to meet you today and discover that you've overcome all that. We wish you every success in what you've undertaken.'

'Am I missing something here?' Steve asked, when Cassandra had gone to greet some other new arrivals. 'What was all that about?'

'Cassandra came to see me about an abortion when she was eighteen. She was always very aggressive and demanding when she came to the surgery, and on the day she referred to I had to tell her that she'd left it too late for an abortion. The result was she went berserk and attacked me. The rest of the staff came and restrained her, then sent for the police and her parents, who knew nothing about the pregnancy. Do you know Jack Leminson at all?'

Did he know Jack Leminson? 'Er…yes. I know him slightly.'

'He's known to be a good builder, but I didn't rate him much of a father during that episode. He was fidgeting to get back to work all the time he was with his wife and daughter and the police.

'But,' she said, lowering her voice, 'some way, somehow that girl has sorted herself out. It is great to see her involved in something like this. She's barely twenty-two, yet look what she's achieved already.'

'And she actually attacked you?'

'Mmm. She was a handful in anybody's book.'

'Is she the reason why you were reluctant to come here today?'

'Well, yes. I didn't want it to turn into a free-for-all, knowing our past history. I haven't seen her for years so wasn't sure what to expect. She moved to a practice in the town and eventually had the baby, a little girl who is adored by all the Leminson family.'

'So your reluctance to come here wasn't anything to do with us, then.'

'No, Steve. It wasn't. Please, don't read things that aren't there into everything I say and do.'

'I'll try not to,' he promised. He was smiling, but deep down he knew they had a long way to go before Sallie would be eager to spend time with him away from the practice. At the surgery and in the apartment they were on mutual home ground with Liam as a focal point, but he wasn't sure if any contact outside that was ever going to be really welcome.

After they'd eaten and congratulated the two young café owners on the quality of the food, Sallie said, 'I've brought some bread with me. Shall we go by the park and feed the ducks? Hannah takes Liam there sometimes and she says he knows how to throw the bread to them, but he's not happy if they come too near his buggy.'

'We'll have to see that they don't, then,' he said. 'If it was warmer, I could row you both around the lake there. But I don't think there would be much pleasure in it today.'

There was a chill wind and grey winter skies above, so they wouldn't be lingering long by the ducks either, but as long as they were together he didn't care where they were.

That night when they were seated by the fire after Liam had gone to sleep, Steve said, 'Did you press charges against the Leminson girl?'

Sallie shook her head. 'No. She was just a mixed-up adolescent who was pregnant and frightened. I wasn't going to take her to court. Sending for the police was enough to bring her up with a jolt. Why do you ask?'

'Why do you think? Everyone in health care is at risk from overwrought and overstroppy patients. I wish I'd been there to protect you.'

'It's all in the past, Steve,' she said distantly. 'I *am* trying to forget those years.'

Janine Gresty's wedding was to take place on a Saturday in November and half the village had been invited.

Philip had insisted that no expense was to be spared, that his condition was going to be ignored on that day and that, God willing, he would be there to take his daughter down the aisle.

'It will be on crutches, I'm afraid,' Steve had told him, 'with Janine holding onto you and Sallie and I hovering, but I feel that you will manage it.'

Outside caterers had been brought in to organise the reception, which was being held at the farm, but the marriage service was to take place in the village church just down the road.

'If anything stops me from giving Janine away, will you do it for me, Steve?' Philip had asked after he'd had a really bad day in the week before the wedding.

'Yes, of course I will,' he'd replied, 'but *you* are going to do it. Don't start losing your determination at the last minute.'

Philip had smiled. 'OK. Don't badger me. Just stay near, that's all.'

'I'll be like a limpet,' he promised, 'and so will Sallie. You'll have two of us watching over you.'

Hannah had offered to have Liam for the day and put him to bed in the evening, so that they could be there for Philip if he needed them, without having to be responsible for the baby at the same time.

When the housekeeper had collected him on the morning of the wedding the two doctors found themselves alone in the apartment and there was an awkward silence

Having Liam around all the time made the uneasiness between them less obvious. He was a focal point for them both and that way they were able to keep their distance from each other.

There had been no real reunion since Steve had come back, just a sliding into a new way of life that was far from the way they'd once been. There'd been no opening up to each other. No new beginnings. How long could they go on like this? she thought achingly.

As the thoughts pierced her mind like spears, Steve appeared at the door of the spare room stripped ready for the shower. He halted when he saw her expression and questioned, 'What's wrong?'

'Nothing,' she said in a low voice. 'I was just thinking how strange it is without Liam.'

'And is that it?' he exclaimed. 'You're looking as if the world is coming to an end because we're going to be without him for a few hours?'

Sallie shook her head. 'No. That isn't it. The real reason I'm looking like this is because I can't believe that the two polite robots who live here are you and I.'

His eyes darkened. 'So what do you propose we do about it? You have the advantage over me, as I'm the one in the wrong.'

'We were both wrong in the way we behaved,' she said quietly. 'I let you walk all over me instead of fighting back, and you were so hurt and angry you couldn't think straight. And where has it got us? Almost three and a half years on we are like strangers. We used to read each other's thoughts, know each other's needs. You had only to touch me and I melted.

We couldn't exist without each other, or so we thought. But we have done, haven't we...existed without each other?'

He took a step nearer and as Sallie felt her blood start to warm he asked, 'What's brought this on?'

She shook her head. 'I don't know. Maybe it's the time of the month.'

'Oh, that! Do you think you would melt at my touch now, Sal, after all we've been through?'

'I don't know,' she whispered. 'It's so long ago. I don't know how I would feel.'

'Are you asking me to make love to you?'

'Do you want to?'

'A needless question if ever I heard one. But do you remember when you shrank away from me, I told you then that I would never touch you again unless you asked me to. That I would have to be sure I wasn't falling into another pit I'd dug for myself.'

'So touch me,' she whispered. 'I'm asking you.'

'Where? Where do you want me to touch you?'

'Anywhere. Just so that I can feel your hands on me.'

'You are just as lovely as ever,' he said huskily. Reaching out for her, he kissed her, stroking the slender curve of her back and the mounds of her buttocks. Then with his arms still around her he led her towards the bed, exultant to know that the magic was still there.

But he was being too optimistic. Sallie was stiffening in his arms, holding herself away from him.

'What is it?' he asked warily.

'I can't!' she cried. 'I'd forgotten what those last few

months of desperate attempts at baby-making were like. I couldn't go through that again. Hoping that my period wouldn't come, and, when it did, dreading having to tell you.'

He released her. 'I've told you that it won't be like that now,' he said flatly. 'I've accepted what happened and put it behind me. But if you've suddenly decided that you need an excuse to refuse me, I'll go and have the shower that I was about to take. In case you've forgotten, we *are* going to a wedding.'

'I'm sorry, Steve,' she said to his departing back. 'I should have known it wouldn't be that easy.'

The arrangement was that they would call at the farm to check on Philip before going to the church, and as they drove the short distance there was silence between them once more.

They had both dressed with care, Sallie in a long beige winter coat with a fur collar and a matching soft wool dress beneath it and Steve in a dark suit with a pristine white shirt and silk tie.

To the uninformed onlooker they would be seen as a striking pair who had everything going for them, with their own medical practice in a beautiful Cheshire village. There'd been a rift some time ago. A bit of a mystery it had been. But from the way that Stephen Beaumont looked at his wife these days, it would seem that it was well and truly behind them.

They wouldn't know that Sallie Beaumont's pleasant

efficiency and her husband's brisk approach to health care concealed the sadness of a marriage gone wrong.

As Sallie gave Steve a quick sideways glance from beneath lowered lids, she thought that he was still the most attractive man she'd ever met. Someone that men envied and women noticed. Yet he had only ever wanted her, average figure, average looks, average everything.

He'd wanted her back there at the apartment, and she'd wanted him, desperately, until the pain of the past had come surging back. Now she was ashamed for creating the moment that had been the last thing in his mind as he'd gone to shower.

They needed to perk up before they got to the Grestys', Steve was thinking. It was Janine's big day, and also a very special occasion for her parents. He was praying that Philip was going to be able to achieve his heart's desire but, whether he did or not, the family wasn't going to want two of their friends arriving as if they were attending a funeral instead of a wedding.

'Forget what happened earlier, Sal,' he said flatly. 'Maybe we've outgrown each other.'

'If *that's* what you think,' she said tearfully, 'would I have asked you to make love to me? It was dread that made me tell you to stop. The dread of us going back to how we were before you went away.'

'I can understand that, but there was a time when you believed what I said. You know I've never lied to you, so why should I start now? *It will not be like it was before.* Trust me.'

The farm had come into view and he swivelled to face her. 'We need to lighten up for the Grestys' sake, Sal. Our problems have been on hold long enough. A little longer won't make any difference.'

Philip was already dressed in a silver-grey suit with matching top hat when they arrived. He looked pale and anxious and Anna told them, 'His speech isn't good this morning. Philip is concerned that when he makes his responses, he won't be able to get the words out.'

'Just take your time,' Sallie told him softly. 'There won't be any rush.'

'And I'll be hovering in case you need me,' Steve told him. 'But you're not going to. You're going to be fine.'

At that moment the bride appeared, serene and beautiful, and Sallie felt tears prick. Despite everything, Janine was embracing the present, and if the future held anything unpleasant she would face it then instead of now, with a man who truly loved her by her side.

Maybe she and Steve could learn something from her. When she looked up she found his gaze on her, dark and questioning, and she began to wish she could turn the clock back to those moments in the apartment when the only thing in their minds had been their need of each other. Yet maybe that was why it hadn't felt right. Would it be possible to rebuild their marriage on just desire?

The church was full of family, friends and well-wishers, with flowers everywhere. When Steve saw the bridegroom with his hair cut short and earring missing, he hid a smile. That was going to bring added pleasure to Anna's day, he thought.

He and Sallie were waiting outside the church when the car with the bride and her father arrived, and as they helped Philip out and made sure he'd got a firm hold on the walking frame that Steve had decided was a better idea than crutches, he began to move slowly forward with his daughter's hand under his elbow.

Relieved that they'd set in motion Philip's dearest wish, the two doctors hurried into the church behind them and settled themselves in a pew at the back to watch a brave man give his daughter away in marriage. Philip managed to make his reply to the vicar's question and in the emotion of the moment Steve took Sallie's hand in his and squeezed it hard.

'Oh! Sorry,' he said, and withdrew his grasp.

'Stop it!' she whispered crossly. 'I hate it when you're apologetic over things that don't matter.'

He was smiling. 'You'd rather I was the bolshy beast of yore.'

'Yes. I mean no.'

Janine was now standing beside her bridegroom. They were about to make their vows, and as Anna stepped forward with a wheelchair Steve moved swiftly to the front of the church and helped her to assist Philip into it.

'I did it,' he said in a low, slurred voice. 'I don't know how, but I did it.'

Bending over him, Steve whispered in his ear, 'Didn't I say you would?'

Swivelling the wheelchair round, he placed it at the

end of the front pew where Anna was sitting and then returned to his own place at the back.

He was holding back tears. Sallie saw them and now it was her turn to take *his* hand in *hers,* but this time there was no wry humour in him. 'I sometimes think there is no justice in this world,' he said, and she nodded.

Steve had helped Anna put Philip to bed and was ready to join Sallie at the reception. When he went into the lounge of the farmhouse he saw that Henry Crabtree had collared her and he groaned.

He wasn't the only one to visit the building site when the opportunity arose. From what she'd said, Sallie had also been viewing what was going on there at some time during the previous week and he hoped that Henry hadn't spotted her there.

When he joined them it appeared that he had, as Sallie said, 'Henry is telling me that he saw me in Bluebell Lane, admiring the house that someone is having built. He is just as curious as we are to know who is going to be living there.'

Not wanting to say anything that might set her thinking, Steve just nodded and helped himself to a glass of champagne from a tray held by a hovering waiter.

Anna appeared beside them at that moment and to his relief the discussion about the house in Bluebell Lane ended.

'Thank you both for helping Philip,' she said. 'It took a tremendous effort on his part, but he got his wish. He gets weaker by the day and I wonder how long we are going to have him with us.'

'It may be longer than you think,' Sallie told her gently. 'The illness will take its course and in its later stages you might be relieved to see him go.'

'That was a bit steep, what you said to Anna,' Steve said as they drove home in what had turned out to be a wet and misty night.

'Anna is a realist,' she said. 'She won't want to be fobbed off with platitudes. She's seeing the man she loves grow weaker all the time and needs to know the score.'

He sighed. 'Yes. I suppose you're right, and, whether Anna knows the score or not, Philip does.'

'If your cancer hadn't been treatable and had run amok, I might have been in the same position as Anna, watching the man I loved dying before my eyes.'

They arrived home and after pulling up in front of the surgery Steve turned to face her. 'Is that your way of saying that I should have been more anxious about the cancer and less fraught about my fading dreams of fatherhood?'

'You should have been concerned about both and been thankful that Tom Cavanagh had cleared you of the cancer. That should have been enough to be going on with, but there was this overpowering need in you to have children and it took over our lives.'

'I thought that you wanted them as much as I did.'

'I did, but I wanted *you* more. All I could think about at that time was that you'd had cancer. That I could have lost you. Nothing else was as important as that.'

Without comment, Steve looked upwards to where the lights of the apartment were shining out in the rain and mist and said, 'Shall we go and see if Liam has missed us?

She smiled. 'I'm hoping that he'll be asleep. It will be strange if he isn't at this time of night.'

'And I'm not allowed to wake him up,' he teased.

'Don't even think about it.'

Hannah was waiting for them at the top of the stairs with a worried expression on her face, and they tuned into it immediately.

'What's wrong?' Steve asked, leaping up the last few steps. 'Is it Liam?'

She shook her head. 'No. He's fast asleep. The vicar's wife has just been on the phone to say that the Scout group from the church were taken on a march across the moors this morning. They should have been back late afternoon but haven't turned up. The vicar has phoned the police and they are going to organise a search party, but the villagers aren't prepared to wait and some of them are ready to go and look for them themselves. They feel that a doctor in the search party would come in handy if any of them have been injured or are suffering from the cold and wet conditions up there.'

Steve went into the bedroom and got out of his wedding clothes. When he reappeared dressed in a thick anorak, jeans and walking boots, he found Sallie dressed in similar clothes.

She saw that he was frowning and told him, 'I'm coming, too. Hannah says she will stay the night with Liam if need be. Are you ready?'

'Yes,' he said abruptly. 'And I don't see the need for you to go. It could be treacherous up there.'

She shook her head. 'You know what they say. Two doctors are better than one, and I know the moors as well as anybody. So let's get moving or they'll be setting off without us. And we need torches, Steve. There are a couple in one of the kitchen cupboards.'

CHAPTER SIX

WHEN they arrived at the church Alison greeted them. It was clear she was trying to keep calm, which wasn't easy under the circumstances as two of her children were among those missing.

The vicar was there and the fathers of some of the Scouts. When they saw the two doctors there were nods of approval. One of the men said, 'Let's hope that we don't need you, but something is wrong up there.' And as they piled into three cars that would take them along the route where the trek was to have taken place, nobody seemed inclined to disagree with him.

Steve had been right about it being treacherous. As they drove higher up the hillside, the mist became thicker and in the end they parked the cars and set off on foot.

Some of them had lamps, others torches, and almost everyone had brought their mobile phones, but they were of little use in the terrain on which they found themselves

Steve was gripping Sallie's hand tightly and he told her, 'Don't budge from my side. We mustn't get separated from each other. I was insane to have agreed to you coming.'

'You couldn't have stopped me.'

She could just about see his face in the swirling mist and there was a half-smile on it. 'No, I don't suppose I could. It's like the old days when we did everything together. But if I had a choice I would prefer an evening at the Kestrel.'

The search party was walking in single file so that each of them had the benefit of the light carried by the person behind, as well as their own. Most of them were well acquainted with the moors and the gullies among them, but progress was being hindered by the extreme weather conditions.

As they trudged along the tops there was a grim silence as words like 'hypothermia' and 'extreme-exhaustion' kept coming to mind. They'd brought flasks of hot drinks with them and everyone had a blanket in their backpack, but they weren't going to be of any use until they found the missing group.

Every time they came to a steep drop they all flashed their torches down to check that there was no one sheltering or lying at the bottom. Remote barns and outbuildings were searched but there was no sign of a group of bedraggled boys and their leader.

'The risks wouldn't be as great on a warm summer night,' Steve said in a low voice that was for Sallie's ears only, 'but it's November. Without protection you could die of exposure up here. I don't suppose they would have had a tent with them.'

They found them at last at the bottom of a deep gully between the peaks. When they saw the faint light of lamps and torches up above the Scouts sent up a cheer, and it was the sweetest sound those searching for them had ever heard.

When they'd made their way carefully to the bottom of the drop and been greeted thankfully by the Scoutmaster, he said, 'We've got a lad here with what is almost certainly a broken leg.' He turned to the worried clergyman. 'It's your son, Jeremy, Vicar. He missed his footing and came hurtling over the edge as the light was fading and we were on our way back to the village.

'We've given what first aid we could,' he went on as they gathered around the injured youth, 'but we need an ambulance and my phone isn't working.'

'I've managed to get through on mine,' Sallie said. 'As soon as I knew we'd found you, I rang the ambulance services to tell them where we were.'

Steve was crouching beside the vicar's son and he said, 'Jeremy is only semi-conscious. There could be a head injury of some sort but in this light it's impossible to tell.' When he'd examined the leg he reported, 'There is a fracture all right, that much I *can* see. There's a first-aid kit in my rucksack, Sallie, with some thick crêpe bandages in it. If you'll strap his legs together, I'll check the rest of him as best I can.'

Sallie turned to the vicar. 'I'm going to strap his legs together, Robert, to avoid further damage when they move him. Then all we can do is sit tight until the emer-

gency services arrive.' She then addressed the
Scoutmaster, 'How long has he been slipping in and out
of unconsciousness?'

'Ever since the fall. He came round just before you
found us and then drifted off again.'

Steve turned to Sallie. 'What do you think?'

'Either a head injury of some kind or shock,' she said.

One of the fathers was hovering and he said, 'We'd like
to get our boys back home. They are wet, tired and hungry.'

Sallie looked around at the rest of the bedraggled
troop and their anxious fathers and she said, 'Yes, of
course. Take your boys home. They need hot baths and
food. We'll be here with the vicar until the ambulance
comes and if you think any of them should be checked
over by Steve or myself when we get home, we'll open
the surgery.'

As the fathers and sons climbed up the steep side of
the gully onto the level ground above, the Scoutmaster
said, 'I'm staying. I was responsible for their safety.
Jeremy was in my care, and if it's all right with you,
Vicar, I'm going with you in the ambulance.'

As Sallie was finishing strapping the boy's legs
together, Steve said, 'We need someone up on the top
to watch out for the ambulance, otherwise they could be
searching for us all night in this sort of weather.'

He checked Jeremy's breathing again, making sure
that his tongue hadn't gone back and was blocking his
airway, and she said, 'I'll go.' Picking up a lamp and a
torch, she set off.

'You aren't going up there on your own. Don't even

think of it!' Steve exclaimed, without looking up from what he was doing. 'It's too dangerous. I don't want to have to come searching for *you*, Sallie.'

When he looked up she wasn't there and he groaned. The mist seemed thicker than ever and all he could hear was her clambering over wet rock and slithering on clay.

'I should have gone,' the vicar choked, 'but I don't want to leave Jeremy. This is my worst nightmare.'

'Mine, too,' the Scoutmaster said wearily and collapsed onto a nearby ledge.

At that moment Jeremy opened his eyes and gave a soft moan. 'Where am I?' he asked. 'What happened?' Then, with a grimace, he said, 'My leg hurts.'

'Thank goodness he's back with us,' his father said, and Steve nodded his agreement.

'It's a good sign,' he said. 'He seems rational enough at the moment and is as warm as we can manage to make him.'

He switched his glance to the mist-covered slope that led to the top of the gully and said, 'I have to check on my wife.'

Unaware that he'd followed her, Sallie was swinging the lights from side to side frantically when he reached the top. He grabbed her from behind and spun her round angrily.

'Are you insane?' he said through gritted teeth. 'My heart almost stopped when I saw that you'd gone after I'd told you not to. Have you got a death wish or something?'

She smiled. 'No. But I did almost die of fright when a big sheep came out of the mist right past me. I'm sorry I caused you worry but I was the obvious one to come back up top to keep a lookout for the ambulance. The vicar wouldn't want to leave his son's side You were needed to keep an eye on his condition, and the Scoutmaster looked completely exhausted...' She trailed off. 'Do I see headlights in the distance?'

'Yes, you do, but they won't be here yet. It's too soon.'

'Not necessarily,' she told him. 'When I made the call I was told that they weren't too far away and I can hear a siren.'

Steve listened. 'Yes, so can I. Thank goodness for that! Once they arrive, please come back to where I can see you. This could have turned into a real tragedy if we hadn't found those boys. I'm going back down now. Jeremy regained consciousness for a few moments and I'm hoping he stays that way. I just wish I had more light to assess his injuries properly. Tell them to position their headlights when they get here so that they shine down as much as possible into the gully.'

Midnight was long gone by the time the two doctors arrived back home, and Hannah was dozing in a chair by the window where she'd been watching out for them.

They'd stopped off at the vicarage to let Robert's agitated wife, Alison, know that Jeremy was on his way to hospital with a possible head injury. Their other son had arrived home with the rest of the Scouts and their fathers, so she was aware of what had happened but desperate for news. When it had come, she'd set off immediately for the hospital.

Steve had explained to the paramedics that Jeremy

was either suffering from severe shock or had suffered a head injury of some sort, which had caused him to lose consciousness.

It hadn't been the easiest of tasks, stretchering him up from the bottom of the gully in those conditions, but it had been achieved at last, and the fact that the injured leg had been strapped to the other had saved any jarring as they'd carried him upwards. But there was still anxiety because of the way he was drifting in and out of consciousness.

When Steve came back from taking Hannah home, Sallie said, 'Are you still annoyed with me for going back up top to watch out for the ambulance?'

He was peeling off his wet clothes and easing his feet out of the heavy boots and paused to tell her unsmilingly, 'I was more concerned than annoyed. It was a nightmare out there, trying to treat the lad under those conditions, and then you disappear.'

It was putting it mildly. The thought of anything happening to her had made him feel sick inside. He supposed that he might have overreacted and was about to discover that, as far as Sallie was concerned, he had.

'Do you honestly think I would have done anything to make matters worse? The directions I'd given in my phone call had been hazy to say the least, and without some guidance the ambulance might not have found us. It was kind of you to be concerned, but who do you think has been watching over me for the past three years, Steve? Nobody!'

His face had whitened. 'I do know that. It was my

mistake. I was presuming too much. I thought that we were at least friends, and I wouldn't want to see a friend in danger. But it seems a shame to be bickering over something like this when the vicar and his family are coping with so much at this moment, don't you think?'

Yes, she did, Sallie thought wretchedly as he went into his room and closed the door. Why couldn't she have accepted Steve's concern for her in the spirit it had been meant? Was there an urge inside her to punish him for what he'd done? She hoped not. It wasn't in her nature, but she *was* still keeping him at a distance and couldn't see that changing until her hurt went away.

They heard the next day that it had been severe shock affecting Jeremy the night before. Apart from cuts and bruises there had been no injuries other than the fracture, and he was now stable.

It was his mother who brought news of him. Alison called on her way home from the hospital to bring them up to date on what was happening, and at the same time thanked them for turning out for him.

'We were only too happy to be of assistance,' Sallie told her. 'I felt so sorry for the three of them. For Jeremy having the nasty accident, for his father for finding him in that state and for the poor Scoutmaster, who was most upset that something like that should have happened when he was in his care.'

'Yes. I know,' Alison said with a shudder. 'But I suppose it could have been worse. I've never seen the effects of severe shock before and it was frightening. However, he's recovering so we have much to be thankful for.'

Steve appeared at that moment with Liam in his arms, and when he too had been brought up to date with the news on Jeremy, he said, 'It was difficult to treat him under those conditions, and I was very much afraid he had a head wound.'

When she was ready to go Alison said, 'What a pity that this little one will soon be leaving the village. It's a great place for bringing up children.'

'We're delighted to say that Liam won't be leaving,' Steve said. 'My niece and her partner are intending to settle down here.'

'Really? That's great news,' she said, and touched Liam's cheek. 'Lucky little boy.'

When she'd gone Sallie went into the kitchen to start the preparations for Sunday lunch, and Steve followed her. 'I'll take Liam out for a while if you like,' he offered. 'It will give you some time to yourself.'

She swivelled round to face him. Her hasty words of the night before hadn't been commented on by either of them since they'd met up at breakfast and she couldn't leave it like that.

'I'm sorry about last night, Steve,' she said in a low voice. 'It was churlish of me to be so ungrateful over your concern. Can you forgive me?'

'There is nothing to forgive,' he said flatly. 'What you said is true. I *wasn't* there for you when you needed me, so why should you have to be grateful now?'

She didn't reply to that. Instead, she said, 'If you'll hang on while I put the joint in the oven, I'll come with you.'

It was a typical November morning, grey and overcast, but as Steve pushed Liam's buggy with Sallie beside him they weren't too aware of the weather. Both had more important things on their minds.

Another difficult moment had passed and they still wanted to be with each other, Sallie was thinking. In Steve's thoughts was the fast-approaching return of Melanie and her boyfriend, and he was wondering what would be left for Sallie and himself once Liam had gone back to his mother. Would the frail bond between them fracture?

She had only once shown any real feeling towards him and that had been on the morning of Janine's wedding, but it had been short-lived because of the past rearing its head. Her reaction when she saw the house would be a good guide to what the future held, and it wasn't going to be long before that happened.

His conversation with Alison about Liam staying in the village must have brought Melanie to Sallie's mind too as she said, 'What about somewhere for Melanie to live? We still haven't sorted it.'

Melanie was due to return during Christmas week and every time Sallie mentioned it Steve assured her that it would all be sorted by the time they arrived.

Christmas was just three and a half weeks away and the house was almost finished. It had been built exactly how Sallie had described her dream house and every time he saw it Steve felt pleasure wash over him. If she

would come to live with him in it, there would be no
need for her to hold his shirt in her arms, he thought.
He would be where he belonged, beside her.

Old Henry had gone to stay with his daughter for
Christmas and the weeks leading up to it, as there wasn't
adequate heating in his cottage, which meant that Steve
was free to visit the site without being observed after
the workmen had finished for the day. The electricity
had been connected and each evening he went to check
on progress, wandering from room to room behind
makeshift curtains.

He wasn't intending to do anything about furnishings. He knew that, provided all went well, Sallie would
want to choose them herself once she'd absorbed the
fact that he and she were the mystery owners of the
house in Bluebell Lane.

But in the midst of his euphoria he did have moments
when panic set in. It made him feel weak at the knees when
he thought of what he would do if she said she'd got used
to the solitary life and wanted to stay where she was.

He was hoping she would see it as a new beginning.
A reunion of minds as well as bodies. It had seemed
claustrophobic in the apartment since he'd come back,
helping to care for Liam while trying to live normally
in a situation that was anything but.

Sallie's curiosity finally got the better of her one evening
when Steve said, as he had on previous occasions, 'I'm
just popping out. I won't be long.'

'Where do you go when you dash off the moment

we've eaten?' she asked. 'If it's to see Philip, why don't you say so?'

'I visit Philip during the day, so I have no need to go in the evening unless I'm sent for,' he told her. 'I'm involved in a project with some of the men in the village. You'll find out what it is soon enough.' And without giving her the chance to question him further, he departed.

Minutes later, as he put his key in the new front door that he hoped Sallie would soon be going in and out of, he hoped he hadn't given the game away.

The next morning, before he was about to start his calls, one of the teachers from the school appeared. 'I haven't come as a patient, Dr Beaumont,' she said, 'but as someone who needs to ask a favour of you.'

As he listened to what she had to say, he started smiling. The smile was still there when Sallie saw him, and he said, 'I've just seen one of the teachers from the school and they want me to be Santa on the day of the nativity play. Apparently Henry Crabtree usually does it, but as he's gone off to his daughter's and none of the other old folk are fit enough, they've asked me.'

'What did you say?' she asked doubtfully.

'I said yes, and I know what you're thinking. It will make me miserable, being with a lot of other people's children.'

'Yes, something like that,' she admitted reluctantly.

'You know, sometimes I think you're disappointed that I'm not pining any more,' he said flatly. 'I'm all right with Liam, aren't I, and the children I treat at the surgery? I can't avoid them because I've got none of my own.' Then his good humour returned. 'Remind me to practise my Ho, ho, hos.'

As he drove along on his rounds, he saw a sprightly Lizzie Drury moving along the pavement, and she waved. He pulled up beside her and, pointing to her leg, she said, 'I've got the dressing off at last, Dr Beaumont. I don't have to go to the clinic any more.'

'That's great news, Lizzie,' he said, and continued on his way to visit a newcomer to the village. The story going around was that seventy-year-old Jennifer Maxwell had been an actress until a fall on stage had caused a serious leg injury that had ended her career.

The house she had moved into had belonged to her brother, Lionel, a reclusive bachelor. He had let what had once been a desirable residence fall into disrepair, and now, according to the village grapevine, the drab place was coming to life. Cobwebs were being swept away and refurbishment had begun.

Steve had never met the woman, but knew she'd signed on with the practice when she'd arrived in the village, and he was looking forward to meeting her.

Breathing difficulty had been mentioned when the request for a visit had been made, and when a receptionist had asked if she could manage to get to the surgery she'd said frostily, 'Definitely not.' And so there Steve was.

Jennifer did not look a happy woman, he thought when she answered the door. There were pain lines around her mouth and a sour expression on her face, but in spite of her age, or maybe because of it, there was a sort of toned-down elegance about her.

'I'm Steve Beaumont, your GP,' he told her, taking note that she was using a stick for support as she stepped back to let him in.

'Yes. I know. I've seen you around the village.' The voice was more pleasant than the expression, he thought.

'And what is the problem?' he asked, above the noise of drilling and hammering in the background.

'I've been coughing up blood and I'm short of breath,' she explained with bleak brevity.

'Let's see what your chest has to tell me,' he said, producing his stethoscope, 'if you wouldn't mind unbuttoning the top two buttons of your blouse.' The woman nodded stiffly and he proceeded to examine her.

'You have a chest infection, Jennifer,' he told her. 'I'm going to put you on a course of antibiotics. As for the blood that you're coughing up, I'll need a sample of sputum brought to the surgery the next time it happens. Then we can send it to be tested.'

Jennifer sighed. 'There's been a horrendous amount of dust and grime flying about since I brought the workmen in, and after a few days I developed a hacking cough.'

'The blood could be from a burst blood vessel in your throat, caused by the severity of the cough,' he commented. 'If that proves to be the case, it's nothing to worry about, but we do need to check it out.'

'All right,' she agreed reluctantly. 'I'll do what you ask.'

'Good. By the way, Jennifer, how are you enjoying country life?' he asked, on the point of leaving.

'I'm not. I was brought up in this mausoleum. I escaped by going to drama school and after that had some good parts. I was on top of the world, having the time of my life, until I had a fall and shattered my leg. The doctors put it all back together again, but it's now shorter than the other and there isn't much call for an actress with a limp.'

'That was tough luck,' he said sympathetically. 'But it doesn't explain why you've come back to your roots, if you don't like country life.'

Jennifer sighed. 'With the loss of my career, my earnings disappeared. The insurance people paid out, but it didn't last for ever. Then my brother left me this place. He'd arranged that there would be enough money to have it repaired, but in his will stipulated that it was only to be used for that purpose. If I didn't come back to live here, the money was to go to charity, which meant that the house would have become even more derelict than it was already. So, you see, I didn't have much choice.'

Steve nodded. 'I get the picture,' he told her. 'But surely you can use your talents in another way? Maybe by teaching drama. Or how about forming a drama group here in the village and putting on a show or a play?'

She managed a wintry smile. 'Is it a regular thing?'

'Is what a regular thing?'

'You dishing out therapy at the same time as pills.'

He smiled back at her. 'It is sometimes. Then again, sometimes I find that I'm the one who needs to be pointed in the right direction.'

'Are you married?' she asked.

'Yes. My wife is the other partner in the practice.'

'Children?'

'No.'

'Well, they can be a nuisance.'

He didn't take her up on that. He knew that lots of theatre folk put their career before all else. Even Melanie, who loved her baby, hadn't been able to resist the pull of the stage.

When he got back to the surgery and told the receptionist who'd tried to save him a visit what the problem had been, she exclaimed, 'The woman could have come to the surgery with that!'

'Yes. I know,' he agreed, 'but I sense that she's depressed and the state of that house is enough to depress anyone. But I've impressed on her that she has to get here with a sample of sputum as soon as possible, and as the car at the front of the house would indicate that she can still drive, there is no reason for her not to do so.'

He didn't tell Sallie about his suggestions regarding Jennifer Maxwell's dramatic talents as he wasn't sure if the old lady would want to do such things, but the more he thought about it, the more he could see a village pantomime or musical taking shape.

'Perhaps we should invite her for a meal some time,' Sallie suggested that evening, when he mentioned his visit to Lionel Maxwell's old house briefly. 'She might feel more as if she belongs when she gets to know some of us.'

Steve smiled across at her. After being with the miserable mistress of the grim house on a remote lane leading to the moors, it was good to be back with the one person he wanted to be with.

The next morning one of the practice nurses reported that the sputum sample had been delivered and had gone off to be checked, and that the woman who'd brought it had looked as if she didn't know how to smile.

There was no denying that Jennifer Maxwell was not a happy woman and with that in mind he mentioned her to the vicar that same day.

Robert Martin was in his forties and whether it be a member of his flock or not, it made no difference to the diligence with which he did his job. If someone was in any kind of need he was there, and when Steve mentioned the lonely, not very mobile woman to him, he immediately said he would call on her and ask if there was any way that he could be of help.

They were an easy, friendly family, Robert, his wife Alison and their two teenage children, and no matter how often the phone rang on parish business, or who appeared on their doorstep, the vicar and his wife were always ready with a listening ear or a helping hand.

When Steve told him that he'd tried to get Jennifer interested in a drama group or something similar, Robert said, 'I'll back you up on that. We have teenagers who hang around with nothing to do in the evenings, and as most folk are always eager to get involved in some sort of drama, this lady could fill a gap in their lives if she is agreeable.'

'That's just it,' Steve explained. 'I don't think that she wants to be agreeable. She's already told me she doesn't like country life so don't be too disappointed if she shows you the door.'

The vicar laughed, unperturbed. 'That's happened to me a few times, I can tell you, but we clergy are thick-skinned. I'll report back when I've bearded the lady in her den.'

When the results on the sputum came back there was no cause for alarm and Steve decided that it must have been as he'd said, a blood vessel that had ruptured due to coughing.

When the receptionist rang Jennifer to give her the good news, the elderly lady asked to speak to him. She told him that the vicar had been to see her, and was there a conspiracy afoot. She just wanted to be left alone, and before he could reply she'd gone off the line.

'Don't give up on her,' Sallie said, when he told her what had happened. 'Leave it for a while and then try again.'

'Whatever,' he agreed absently. They'd just finished eating and he was anxious to pay his nightly visit to the new house.

The nativity play was a huge success. The hall of the village school was packed with parents and grandparents, keen to see their offspring in whatever role they had been given to play.

When the performance was over there was an

interval, and Steve went to get dressed for his part in the proceedings, which was to be coffee and mince pies for the adults and presents from Santa for the children.

While he was away Sallie looked around her and her glance rested on a woman sitting in the back row of the school hall in the seat nearest to the door.

She guessed immediately that it was Jennifer Maxwell, from Steve's description of her. It would seem that the school's amateur attempt at drama had brought the elderly actress out of her shell, she thought as she moved towards her through the crowd.

'I'm the other Dr Beaumont,' she said with a friendly smile. 'I believe you've already met my husband.'

'Yes, I have,' she said, without returning the smile. 'He and the vicar want to integrate me into village life.'

'I can recommend it,' Sallie said. 'I'm so glad that you decided to join us tonight. The folk here are a friendly lot and on these sort of occasions most of those in the audience are connected with one of the children in some way or another.'

'Yes. So I believe,' the actress said, without any noticeable softening. 'He said that you and he hadn't got any family, but I've seen you both out with a baby.'

'That's Liam, my husband's niece's son. We are looking after him while his mother is working abroad. Our housekeeper, Hannah, is minding him for us tonight.' And having no wish to discuss that angle of their private affairs any further, she changed the subject by asking, 'Are you going to join us for mince pies and coffee? Steve is Santa and is looking forward to giving out presents to the children.'

But it seemed as if attending the play was to be the extent of Jennifer's venture into village life, as she shook her head and said, 'No, thanks. I have to get back. I'm expecting a phone call.' And on that note she limped out into the winter night.

Steve never did anything by halves. Santa he had been asked to be, and Santa he was as he took the youngest children onto his knee and listened to their bemused requests for Christmas morning deliveries, and when the older children of the primary school, who were less in awe of him, had their moment, he bent an attentive ear, not forgetting his 'ho, ho, hos' at regular intervals.

Sallie found herself smiling as she watched him. The children had no idea that Santa was Dr Beaumont who sounded their chests and took their temperatures when they were poorly. For just this short time he was for them that other focal point of Christmas.

They'd done the baby-in-the-manger bit with the shepherds and wise men, and now their thoughts were on what Santa was going to bring them on Christmas morning. Somehow Sallie didn't think they would be asking for gold, frankincense or myrrh.

'I met Jennifer Maxwell tonight,' Sallie told him when they were back home beside the fire.

'You mean to say she was at the play?'

'Yes.'

'I don't believe it! The last time I spoke to her she said she wanted to be left alone. So maybe the vicar and I have got through to her and she's ready to drop the Greta Garbo thing.'

'She isn't the easiest of people to get to know, is she? It was hard work, trying to make her thaw out, and I don't really feel that she did in the end.'

'You've described her exactly, but I'm sure she'll come round eventually. The fact that she's turned up at the only dramatic-type evening we've had in ages is a good sign.'

'I think that she relates to you more than me,' Sallie said. 'She wasn't exactly beaming her approval when she met me. Maybe she thought your wife would have been more spectacular.' She was laughing when she said it but he didn't join in.

'I don't care what anyone else thinks. It's whether *you* still think you're right for me that matters. Do you? Or have I really blown it?'

She didn't meet his glance. 'I don't know.'

'You sleep with one of my old shirts in your arms.'

Her face flamed. 'How do you know that?'

'You kept crying out in your sleep one night and I went to see if you were all right. I saw it then, and have wondered ever since what could have been the reason for your distress.'

'I've no idea,' she said shortly. 'I must have been agonising over something in my dreams.'

She was saved further embarrassment as cries from the bedroom informed them that Liam was awake, and

Steve was on his feet immediately. When he brought Liam into the sitting room there were two spots of bright red colour on his cheeks and the tears were flowing fast. He was teething and not liking it.

'I suggest that one of us gives him something for the pain in his gums, followed by a dry nappy and some gentle cuddling,' he said, 'and that the other makes some tea.' He was smiling again. 'One sugar for me, Sal.'

CHAPTER SEVEN

THEY hadn't had many disturbed nights with Liam, but the one that followed was in a class of its own. There was a tooth almost through and it was hurting, no matter what they did.

Every time they'd soothed him off to sleep he awoke the moment they laid him in his cot and started crying again. At three o'clock in the morning Steve said whimsically, 'Wrap him up warm, Sallie, and I'll take him for a drive. That usually does the trick, and I won't come back until he is in a deep sleep.'

She flashed him a tired smile. 'All right, but don't be too long. It will soon be time to start another day.'

'I know that all too well,' he told her, 'and while I'm away get some sleep yourself.'

When he'd started the car she carried Liam carefully down the stairs and fastened him into the baby seat. As Steve prepared to drive off, she shivered in the night air and, pulling her robe more tightly around her, told him, 'This is crazy, but I'm coming with you.'

'Not as crazy as him crying all night,' he said. 'Liam

will be out like a light as soon as he feels the movement of the car. But there's no need for you to come. Go to bed while you have the chance, Sallie.'

She was opening the car door and slipping into the passenger seat. 'I wouldn't go to sleep if I did. Not with you driving Liam around the neighbourhood as a last resort. Tonight would have been horrendous if I'd been on my own. I'm so glad to have you around on these sorts of occasions.'

If it had been a calmer moment, instead of with Liam's cries ringing in his ears, he might have asked, And what about the rest of the time? And maybe got the kind of answer he didn't want.

He had been right. Liam closed his eyes and went to sleep almost immediately, but Steve wasn't going to turn back, not until he was really settled. As he drove around the village all was still, no signs of life anywhere. Suddenly out of the blue a police car came from a side road and waved him down.

He stopped and wound down the window and one of the two officers who had stopped him asked, 'Might I ask where you are going, sir, and can I see your licence?'

'We're not going anywhere in particular,' Steve said as he passed his licence over. Before he could explain further, Liam woke up and began to cry once more.

'There's your answer, officer. We've got a teething baby in the back who just won't go to sleep, so in desperation we're taking him for a drive. Does that satisfy you?'

'Yes, sir,' he said with a grin. 'I've been there myself

a few times. It is just that cars driving slowly around the neighbourhood at this time of night are sometimes up to no good.' And he waved them off.

Liam's wails subsided when the car moved off again, and, glancing across at Sallie, Steve rolled his eyes heavenwards. It was hilarious to be suspected of being burglars while dressed in their nightwear with coats flung over the top and a teething baby in the back of the car. She was laughing and he joined in.

By the time they arrived back at the apartment Liam was well and truly asleep and as they gently laid him in his cot, still wrapped in the blanket, the clock on the bedside table said five o'clock.

'No use going back to bed,' Steve said, when they'd closed the door quietly behind them. 'We would be having to get up within the hour. Do you fancy a game of Monopoly?' And she dissolved into laughter once more.

Sallie wasn't laughing as the day wore on, though. By the time the afternoon surgery was over she was beginning to feel the effects of their sleepless night, and when Steve came up to the apartment she was yawning while Liam was whizzing around happily in his baby walker.

'Are we to take it that the tooth has come through?' he said.

'He won't let me look at the moment,' she told him, 'but in view of his good humour, I think it must have.'

'Thank goodness for that.'

'Yes, indeed,' she agreed. 'The moment that Liam is

settled for the night, I'm off to bed. You'll have the place to yourself.'

'I might do the same,' he told her, 'but I have to pop out first.'

Sallie woke up suddenly from a deep sleep and saw from the clock that it was two in the morning. At the same moment she realised that it was the telephone in the hall beside her bedroom door that had woken her up.

Before she could get to it Steve had answered and she heard him say, 'I'll be there as soon as I've got some clothes on.'

She was out of bed in a flash. The call had to be connected with Philip Gresty. He was the only person Steve was available to out of hours. Anyone else would have to ring the emergency doctor service.

He was replacing the receiver when she appeared in the doorway of her bedroom, heavy-eyed and wraith-like in a white cotton nightdress.

'Is it Philip?' she asked.

He nodded. 'He's having breathing problems and Anna says his oxygen has almost run out. They've sent for an ambulance, but I want to see him for myself.'

'Have you had any sleep?'

'Yes.' He was grabbing his bag. 'I'll see you when I see you.' As he ran down the stairs he called over his shoulder, 'I hope I don't get stopped by the police again.'

He was back within the hour and found her seated at the kitchen table, sipping at a mug of tea. As she observed him questioningly he said, 'They've admitted

Philip to hospital after stabilising his breathing with a fresh supply of oxygen. It's just to be on the safe side. He'll probably be back home tomorrow.'

'I said I would go with him, but Anna and Janine were by his side in the ambulance and, as we are both aware, the A and E don't like all the neighbourhood turning up.'

He cast a troubled glance in her direction. 'You've had another disturbed night again, haven't you? I'm sorry.'

'Don't apologise for being there for that poor man,' she protested gently. 'Sit down and I'll make you a drink. What would you like?'

'Nothing, thanks,' he said sombrely. 'I'm ready to hit the sack again and I'm sure you are, too. Is Liam all right?'

She nodded. 'Yes. Sleeping the sleep of the innocent.'

He was moving towards the spare room and she didn't want him to go. She could tell he was in low spirits, and she wanted to hold him close and show him that she hadn't stopped caring, but the door was closing behind him. The moment was lost, and she wasn't sure how she would have handled it if it hadn't been.

She'd already done Steve no favours with the way she'd behaved on the morning of the Gresty wedding, almost begging him to make love to her and then changing her mind at the last moment.

He was still in a sombre mood at breakfast and the desire to offer comfort was still there if he would tell her what was wrong. Steve was a positive thinker, not a man of moods, but something was getting to him.

Maybe it was Philip's condition that was upsetting

him, or perhaps something she had said or done. The week that had started well with the nativity play had deteriorated with Liam's teething problems and Steve being called out to his friend in the middle of the night.

They needed some brightness in their lives. A visit to the theatre or a good film at the cinema maybe. But there was Liam to consider, and when Hannah had been at the apartment all day, it was too much to ask her to come back in the evening.

There was no one else she would trust with Melanie's child and she knew that Steve would feel the same way. Their sense of responsibility was strong and, that being so, they would be staying put.

The decision was sidetracked almost before it was made when Hannah arrived with a handful of tickets she was trying to sell for a beetle drive in the village hall that evening.

Steve had already gone down to the surgery, so it was to Sallie that she said, 'It's not in my line. But if you and Dr Beaumont would like to go, I'll come round to mind young Liam.'

It would be a far cry from the theatre or the cinema, Sallie thought, throwing dice and waiting for a six to start making a drawing of a beetle, but it might cheer Steve up to get out of the apartment for a couple of hours.

'Yes, we'll have a couple of tickets,' she told her. 'As long as you don't mind babysitting.'

When the two doctors went upstairs at lunchtime Sallie said to Steve, 'How do you fancy hitting the high spots tonight?'

'I'm not with you,' he told her. 'What do you mean?'

'I've got two tickets for a beetle drive at the village hall. Hannah says she'll babysit for us and I thought a few hours away from our responsibilities would be relaxing, as you seem to be down in the dumps.'

'I am feeling a bit low,' he admitted, 'but there's no call for you to concern yourself. The problem is entirely mine.'

'So what is it?'

'The usual thing. Regrets and frustration. When I saw the state of Philip last night it was brought home to me how important it is to make the most of every moment of every day, instead of looking for somewhere to hide in when things go wrong. Thanks for taking pity on me, but I think I'll give the beetle drive a miss.'

A couple of days later they woke up to dire warnings on television and radio of severe weather on its way, but, with the keys to the dream house jangling in his pocket, Steve barely heard them.

The night before, when the workmen had gone and the site had been cleared, he had met Jack there and the builder had officially handed over the keys.

'We only finished the lily pond and the gazebo at lunchtime,' Jack had told him, and as he'd looked around him he'd said, 'Your wife is a very fortunate woman, Dr Beaumont. I know that mine would love a place like this. But I'm always so busy building houses for other folk, I never find the time to build one for us. We're still living in the semi we bought twenty-five years ago when we got married.'

* * *

Sallie had watched Steve depart into the night quite unaware that he'd been hoping it would be the last time that he disappeared without explanation. He'd intended taking her round to the house the next day and carrying her over the threshold. After that he would be holding his breath.

When he'd gone she decided that in his absence she would wrap the Christmas gifts she'd bought for him. Among them was a watch that he'd admired in the window of the jeweller's in the village and a telescope that she knew he was interested in.

Neither of them were mind-blowing choices. She knew that the only thing he wanted from her was herself, and so far she hadn't been able to give it. She'd been so near to it on the morning of Janine Gresty's wedding, but memories had got in the way.

And now it was going to be the strangest Christmas of their married life. The three previous ones had been non-events because they'd been separated. Would this one be any different? They were back together, but in every way that mattered they were still apart.

When she'd heard him come back from wherever he'd been, she'd pushed the gifts back into the cupboard unwrapped, and her dejection had been replaced by irritation, because for some reason Steve had come back with a satisfied smile on his face.

As they listened to the weather forecast, it was one of the mornings when she wasn't sorry to be living above

the surgery, as outside there was sleet and a biting wind.
Roads and pavements were icy and snow was on its way.

'Try not to be too long on your house calls,' Steve
said. 'There's somewhere I want to take you in the
lunch-hour.'

'Are you serious?' she exclaimed. 'Have you seen
the weather?'

'Yes, I have, but we won't be going far.' And that was
it, as it was almost time for Hannah to appear, and Liam
had just dropped his empty cereal dish over the side of
his high chair. But it left her curious and she wondered
if Steve was going to show her the mysterious accommodation he'd found for Melanie and her family.

Margaret Chalmers, who owned a craft shop in the
village, was Sallie's first patient that morning, and when
she'd seated herself the two women exchanged smiles,
though Margaret's was rather tense.

'Your receptionist phoned to say that you've got
the results back from the tests,' she said without
wasting any time.

'Yes, we have,' Sallie told her, not happy about what
she had to say next, 'and they show that the tendency
towards breast cancer that runs in your family is there
in you, Margaret.'

It was like the Janine Gresty scenario all over again,
she thought. Except for the fact that Janine was in no
hurry to know. She watched the colour drain from
Margaret's face and wished that what she'd had to tell
her could have been different, but it had to be said.

'Your sister was wise to persuade you that you should both be tested to see if either of you are at risk. The results show that she is clear of the inherited genetic abnormality but you have it, and there is a strong possibility that at some time in your life you may develop breast cancer.'

'I didn't want to go for the tests,' Margaret said tearfully, 'but she wouldn't let it rest, and now she has peace of mind and I'll be living in dread.'

'It doesn't have to be like that, Margaret,' Sallie told her gently. 'Just because you've discovered this, it doesn't mean that you are going to get breast cancer. Now that we know the score, you'll be asked to go for regular checks, which means that at the very first sign of anything we'll be on your case.'

The woman seated across from her was in her fifties, pleasant, hard-working, with two grown-up sons and a husband who was the local policeman. Sallie thought that from this moment Margaret's life was going to change, but only if she let it.

She hoped that when she had calmed down Margaret would realise the wisdom of having the tests and feel more positive. That she would see herself as fortunate, rather than unlucky, to be living in an age when such safeguards were available.

'I'm not going to tell my boys about this,' she said as she got up to go. 'No point in blighting their young lives.'

'No point in blighting yours either,' Sallie told her. 'It might never happen. But if it should, the appropriate medical services will be at your disposal.'

Margaret nodded sombrely. 'Thanks for helping me to face up to it. The next thing I must do is speak to my sister. I don't want her having a guilt trip over this.'

'Yes, do that,' Sallie agreed, 'and don't forget, you know where to find me if you need me.'

'You're looking very serious,' Steve said when he came into her room shortly afterwards while searching for a patient's records. 'Was that Margaret Chalmers I saw going out a few moments ago?'

'Yes. I have just had to tell her she has a high risk of getting breast cancer, and it reminded me of what you said when you'd been to visit Philip the other night. That we should grasp each day as it comes. That life is to be lived one day at a time. Yesterday, whether good or bad, has been and gone, and tomorrow has yet to come.'

'Very philosophical,' he commented wryly. 'Did I say that? And which one of us does that apply to?'

Her smile was meant to be reassuring as she told him, 'You said something of the sort. Maybe there's a message in it for both of us.'

'Maybe,' he said, and went back to his patients.

He intended calling at the Grestys' after surgery as Philip was home from hospital and his tomorrows weren't looking very good at all. Swallowing and breathing were getting to be more difficult for him and he was confined to a wheelchair all the time now. It was frustrating that he could do so little for the man, but Anna knew that he would be there in a flash if they needed him, as had been the case a couple of nights ago.

* * *

Sallie had just seen off her last patient and was having a quick coffee before starting her calls when one of the receptionists came in to say that there'd been a call from Jennifer Maxwell to say she'd had a fall and would Dr Stephen Beaumont call to see her.

'Not Dr Sallie Beaumont,' the receptionist commented laughingly. 'It would seem that our elderly actress friend likes your husband. He left twenty minutes ago, and asked us to tell you that he'll be back as soon as he can.'

Sallie frowned. In keeping with the weather forecast, the sleet had turned to snow. Big white flakes had been falling steadily for the last two hours and were turning the village into a winter wonderland. Beautiful to the eye, but a danger to anyone out on the tops, and Jennifer Maxwell's house was high up there in a remote lane.

There were no workmen in sight when Steve arrived, just high white drifts that the wind had blown up to doors and windows. He was going to have to move some of the snow before he could get into the house.

He had a shovel and a blanket in the back of the car, which he always carried in case he was ever trapped in this kind of weather while out on his rounds, and with speed and efficiency he began to shovel the snow away so that Jennifer would be able to get out if she had to, and he would be able to get in.

He saw that she was watching him from one of the windows and thought that at least she appeared to be on her feet. Snow shifting didn't come within the remit of the country GP, he thought wryly, but somebody had to keep their eye on Jennifer.

'I was coming down the stairs and tripped over the cord of my dressing-gown on the last two steps,' she told him as he opened the door and let in a blast of cold air. 'I think I might have fractured my elbow.'

She was holding her left arm across her waist in a bent position and he could see without touching it that the elbow didn't look right.

Still in the offending dressing-gown and nightdress, she was ashen-faced and shivering, either from cold or shock, or maybe both, as the house didn't feel very warm inside. He glanced out of the window. The snow was drifting up against the walls and doors again and he needed an ambulance.

'I'm going to send for the emergency services,' he told her. 'They will take you to A and E for X-rays, and I'm going to ask them not to send you home until they've checked that your house is accessible. The gritters are out on the side roads as well as the main ones, but up here is something else. We'll just have to hope they can get through.'

'And what if they can't?'

'We'll have to play it as it comes,' he told her, as his dream of showing Sallie the house began to fade. Bringing his thoughts back to the present, he examined her elbow, and put the injured arm into a sling before asking, 'Have you had any breakfast?'

Jennifer shook her head. 'No. I'd only just got up and was coming downstairs to make a cup of tea.'

'I see.'

He would have liked to have made her one, she looked as if she could do with it, but if they had to operate, the fact that she'd had no food or drink since the previous night would speed up the process.

'I'm going to go and take a blanket off your bed to wrap round you,' he said as she continued to shiver, 'and perhaps, with a hot-water bottle tucked inside it, you will get warm.'

She managed a grimace of a smile. 'I suppose country life does have its advantages,' she called after him as he climbed the stairs. 'When one's GP is like you.'

The ambulance did get through, but it took half an hour and by that time the colour had come back to the injured woman's cheeks.

'We mustn't linger,' the older of the two paramedics said after Steve had explained why he'd sent for them, 'or we'll be snowed in here and so will you, Dr Beaumont, if you don't get moving.'

'Yes. I know,' he said flatly.

This was to have been the day he gave Sallie her dream house and if he didn't look sharp he could be stranded miles from anywhere in what was turning into a blizzard.

The paramedics had put Jennifer on a stretcher before carefully transferring her to the ambulance. While they were doing that, Steve saw that the key was in the front door. He locked it quickly and dropped it into the pocket of her dressing-gown, submerged beneath the blanket.

'I'll ring A and E tonight to find out what they've

done about your arm,' he told her. 'They might have to operate, and if they do Sallie and I will be in to see you.'

Still a woman of few words, she nodded then was gone. Now it was his turn to make a quick back track to civilisation, but it wasn't that easy. For the first mile he drove in the tracks that the ambulance had left in the snow, but when he came to where it had turned off, heading for the town and the nearest hospital, he was onto deep unbroken snow and the engine stalled.

While Steve was deciding what to do, with the snow continuing to fall relentlessly and his car refusing to budge, Sallie had just got back from visiting a young mother with a new baby girl who was having trouble breast-feeding. Her breasts were very sore, to the extent that she dreaded feeding time, yet at the same time was frantic because the baby wasn't putting on any weight.

The midwife had been to see her and advised that she should persevere, which hadn't surprised Sallie as Joan Adams was fanatically keen for all mothers to breast-feed. But as far as she, Sallie, was concerned, it should be what was best for mother and baby, and after observing the extreme tenderness of the young woman's breasts and taking note of angry little fists waving from the baby's crib, she suggested, 'Give her a bottle for a day or two until your breasts are less painful. In that time the milk will increase so that when she goes back on the breast she will be satisfied. If you find there is too much milk accumulating, express it and put it in the fridge to give to the baby at alternate feeds.'

'You must think I'm stupid,' the worried mother said tearfully.

'Not at all. Some mothers have no trouble with breast-feeding, but for others it's a nightmare. When I get back to the surgery I'll have a word with the midwife and tell her what I've advised you to do.'

'She won't like it.'

'Your welfare and the baby's come before an outsider's personal preferences. How often have you seen her since the birth two weeks ago?'

'A few times, but she can never stay long. She has a heavy workload.'

Haven't we all? Sallie thought wryly, but she was aware that Joan needed extra help from the authorities and she wasn't getting it.

Sallie expected Steve to be waiting for her when she got back to the surgery, but his car wasn't there and neither was he. It was almost two o'clock. If he wanted to take her on this mysterious errand before late surgery, he would have to hurry, she thought.

When she gazed upwards, the peaks looked dark and menacing against a heavy grey sky, and stirrings of unease started. It wasn't that long ago that they'd been up there with the missing Scouts. The weather had been nightmarish then, but that would be as nothing compared to blizzard conditions.

'Have we heard from Steve?' she asked the staff, and was told, no, he hadn't rung in.

At that moment a farmer with a four-wheel-drive came in to pick up a prescription that he needed urgently. He said that the snow was drifting fast in lanes and gullies near the tops and that he was keen to get home before the way was blocked.

'Folk have been known to freeze to death up there in this sort of weather if their cars have got stuck,' was his parting shot, and Sallie shuddered.

'Try Jennifer Maxwell's number for me, will you?' she said to the receptionist, and was told that the line was dead, which could mean that the snow had brought the wires down.

When he hadn't appeared by the time late surgery was due to start, Sallie rang the police and told them Steve had gone to visit a patient on a remote lane up near the tops at twelve o'clock that morning and hadn't returned yet. His mobile phone gave no response.

She was asked to give them full details of his car and the address that he'd gone to and was told they would look into it, which did little to calm her fears.

Sallie knew that what the farmer had said was true. The peaks surrounding the village were majestic, but they could be cruel, too, scorning the frailties of man.

As she put on a calm front for those attending the late surgery, fear made her blood run cold. She loved Steve now more than she'd ever done, she thought achingly. Loved him for the way he'd endured her coolness towards him, and for the way he'd faced up to the curiosity of patients and friends. If anything had happened to him, she would never forgive herself for not telling him how much she cared.

She'd tried to be as supportive as possible during that

terrible time long ago, but the fact remained that *he* had been the one who'd faced the nightmare of cancer and the fear of not being able to father children.

After facing his demons alone, he had come back to her, and what had she done? Kept him at a distance. Let him think she didn't want him any more. He'd heard her crying in her sleep and had found her holding something that had belonged to him. It must have given him hope. But the way she'd reacted when he'd told her what he'd seen would have made him think again.

She rang the police again as soon as she was free, but they had nothing to tell her except that weather conditions up on the tops were atrocious and they would be in touch as soon as they had some news.

Suppose Steve was buried beneath the snow somewhere, or had skidded down a steep hillside. How long would it take for them to discover something like that? she wondered as she climbed the stairs to the apartment with dragging feet.

Hannah met her at the door with Liam in her arms and, on seeing her expression, asked, 'What is it? What's wrong?'

'Steve went up on the tops this morning to visit a patient and he hasn't come back. I've been on to the police and they're dealing with it, but with this kind of weather I'm very concerned.'

It seemed as if Hannah had nothing to say and when Sallie observed her questioningly she said uncomfortably, 'It has happened before, hasn't it?'

'What?'

'That he's gone.'

'Not under these circumstances!' she cried. 'Have you seen what it's like out there, Hannah? And it will much worse over the moors.'

'Yes. I know,' was the reply, but Hannah wasn't looking her in the eye and Sallie thought it was incredible that this woman who knew them so well could think such a thing. It added to her distress.

Yet she couldn't deny the truth of what Hannah had said. Steve *had* left her before, but not without a word. On that other occasion all he'd been short of had been a fanfare of trumpets. Sneaking off was not his style.

After Hannah had gone, the night slid slowly by, with Liam asleep and herself becoming more agitated by the minute. If there was no news by morning she was going to go and search for him herself, she decided desperately. She knew the lanes and gullies up there as well as anybody.

But suppose she found him and it was too late? she told herself, with the memory clear in her mind of what the farmer had said when he'd come for his prescription. Hannah's comments came back to haunt her. Or she didn't find him at all because he didn't want to be found?

There had been all those nights when he'd gone out without saying where he was going. Had he given up on her at last and found someone else? She shook her head. No. He would have told her if he had. There wasn't a deceitful bone in his body.

At five o'clock in the morning there was a ring on the doorbell and she was down the stairs in a flash, but it was only a young constable looking cold and pinched, who'd been sent to tell her that the search was continuing. That Mountain Rescue had been out all night, so far without success, and might soon have to call off the search as the weather was worsening around the peaks.

'It can't get any worse surely,' she cried. 'And what about the patient my husband went to see? Her phone is dead and I'm concerned about what has happened to her as well as him.'

'That question I can answer for you,' he said, as she led him upstairs into the warmth. 'During our enquiries someone living on the lower hillside reported seeing an ambulance going up to the tops late yesterday morning, and when we rang A and E we were told that a Jennifer Maxwell had been admitted with a fractured elbow.'

'The paramedics who'd gone out on the call confirmed that it had been Dr Beaumont who'd sent for them. That he had been alive and well when they'd left him and ready to make a quick departure before he got stuck up there. Apparently he'd locked up the lady's house and given her the key, which could have proved to be unfortunate, as he could have gone inside to shelter if it had been too bad for him to drive back here. The search party made it to the house, but there was no sign of Dr Beaumont or his car.

'I want to join the search party,' she told him desperately.

He shook his head. 'I don't think so. Just stay put. The moment we have anything to tell you, we'll be in touch.'

So Steve had got as far as Jennifer's house, she thought when the constable had gone, and had arranged for her to be taken to A and E. But what had happened after that?

* * *

As she gave Liam his breakfast her eyes were on the closed door of the spare room. If only it would open and he would come striding out, she thought. She would tell him how much she still loved him. How life without him had no meaning. But was it too late? Had she dallied until the opportunity had gone?

When Hannah arrived, her first words were, 'Any news?'

'Yes, and no,' Sallie told her. 'The police have established that Steve arrived at the patient's house and had her transferred to hospital, but no one knows what happened after that.'

'I'm sorry about what I said yesterday,' Hannah said sombrely. 'It was just that I felt for you so much when he left you that I had to warn you it might have happened again. It was a cruel thing he did to you.'

'Steve had cancer, Hannah,' Sallie informed her. 'He was operated on and now might not be able to have children. He was in a state of great despair.'

'But none of us knew that!' Hannah exclaimed. 'We would have all thought better of him if we had.'

'Yes. I know,' Sallie said softly. 'Yet that was how he wanted it to be, and it's why I've never told anyone. But after yesterday I thought that you should know.'

'What a mess, Sallie.'

'It was, but it won't be any more if the peaks haven't claimed him,' she vowed.

CHAPTER EIGHT

WITH the car out of action, Steve decided that the only thing to do was walk with shovel in hand. He was wearing a thick suede jacket and boots, but they were lightweight as he'd had no premonition that the weather was going to worsen so quickly. Within minutes his feet were soaking wet.

Walking was not a good idea, he decided, and turned to go back to the car, which was gradually disappearing beneath the snow. The blanket that he always carried was there, wrapped in plastic to keep it dry, and he found a bar of chocolate in the glove compartment. Then he wondered what to do next.

As he peered through the swirling white mass, he saw a derelict barn in the field beside him and with the blanket in one hand, the shovel in the other, and his feet freezing in the wet boots, he fought his way to the barn and pushed back the sturdy wooden door.

It was cold inside but dry, with straw scattered around and a musty smell of animals, but in his moment of need it was a palace. The first thing he did was take off the wet boots and socks. He sat on the straw and wrapped his feet in the blanket.

Having done what he could towards survival he thought dismally that Sallie would be wondering where he was, and what it was he'd wanted to show her.

He hoped she wouldn't do anything so crazy as to come looking for him. It was weather that he hadn't seen the like of in a long time, and what might have happened if he hadn't seen the barn was a thought not to be dwelt on.

After a while, as his body heat started to rise, he began to feel drowsy and knew it was from fighting his way through the snow to this place. He tried to throw the feeling off, but it was no use. As the snow drifted around his shelter he slept, after telling himself that he may as well because there was nothing else to do. His mobile wasn't picking up a signal and there had been no other signs of civilisation out there, as far as he'd been able to see.

There was tension in the air when Sallie went downstairs to face the day. All the staff were aware that Steve was missing and, because of the village grapevine, so were most of the patients waiting to be seen.

After the constable's warning not to go up amongst the peaks herself she had reluctantly decided to stay put for the time being and keep the practice functioning. It was what Steve would want her to do, but she wasn't sure how long she was going to be able to keep it up.

One of the first of those waiting to be seen was Jack

Leminson, the builder. His car had skidded on the ice the previous night and he'd wrenched his neck.

After she'd examined the affected area, Sallie could tell that he was expecting her to suggest a collar, but she told him that the routine had changed. Recent results had shown that the collar support sometimes did more harm than good and that the neck strain usually went after a while.

'All right,' he said. 'But what if it doesn't go? I'm in the building trade and won't be able to work if it's painful.'

'See how it goes, and if it doesn't clear up, come back,' she told him. 'You *have* got some neck strain, but I don't see it as serious at this moment.'

He hesitated on the point of leaving, and she wondered what was coming next. 'So has he taken you there yet?' he asked.

'Has who taken me where?'

'Your husband. Has he shown you the—?'

'My husband has been missing up on the moors since yesterday,' she interrupted tearfully, and his jaw sagged.

'Oh, heck!' he groaned. 'What a mess! I didn't know that he was the one they were talking about in the waiting room. I heard them say they were searching for somebody lost in the blizzard, but I didn't know who.'

'Yes, well, now you do,' she told him bleakly, and without explaining the question he'd asked he went, his expression revealing his feelings.

It was the longest day Sallie had ever known. There were a couple of calls from the police to say no luck so far and that was it. She skipped lunch as there were two lots of house calls to do and in the snow they were going to take longer than usual. Then there would be the whole of the late surgery patients to attend to.

She didn't know how she was coping, but she was, probably because she knew it was what Steve would want her to do, but by the time the day was over she'd had enough. If they didn't find him soon, she shuddered to think what the outcome might be, and beneath the dread and anxiety was the regret that was tearing her apart because she hadn't told him how much she still loved him.

It was only a matter of days to Christmas, she thought as she climbed the stairs wearily. Soon Melanie would arrive to claim her baby.

It was going to hurt, parting with Liam, but what sort of a Christmas would it be without Steve? What sort of a *life* would it be without him? She'd been without him before, but had known that he was alive somewhere. This could be so different, achingly, heartbreakingly different.

It had stopped snowing at last. Daylight was almost gone. But the glistening white mass all around them was giving off enough glare for the search party to make out the top of a dark blue car sticking out of a drift beside a hedgerow.

A halt was called and with shovels at the ready the would-be rescuers began to clear the snow from around it, stopping only when they saw that the car was empty and the door unlocked

'The doc must have set off on foot,' one of them said

after they'd found his driving licence in the glove compartment. 'A risky thing to do under these circumstances, but I know Stephen Beaumont. He's not the type to do anything daft.'

At that moment the door of an old barn in the middle of the field nearby was pushed slowly open against the snow that had drifted against it, and a voice called out, 'Hey there! Am I glad to see *you*.'

'Didn't I tell you?' the man who'd just spoken said, adding to Steve, 'Hang on there. We'll come and dig you out.

'Phone for an ambulance,' he told one of the team, when they'd cleared the way to the barn and were gathered around Steve, but Steve protested that he would be all right as soon as he'd got some dry footwear.

'OK. You're the doctor,' he was told. 'You'll know the signs of hypothermia as well as we do, and we've got some spare boots in the truck.'

He had woken up late in the evening of the previous day. The cold had brought him out of sleep and he'd known immediately that he had to get his body heat up again or he would freeze. He'd been able to see through the window of the barn that it had still been snowing, which had meant that it had been too dangerous to go out into the night without suitable footwear or proper equipment. So he'd spent the long hours doing exercises and trying not to think how hungry he was, having eaten the chocolate long ago.

What was Sallie doing? he'd wondered. He'd been so

keen to take her to see the house, but it had all gone wrong. He hadn't risked going to sleep again in case he missed anyone searching for him or developed hypothermia.

When he'd heard the voices of the mountain rescue team it had been like music to his ears, and when he'd forced the barn door open and hailed them across the snow they'd looked like an expedition on Everest.

And now they were taking him back to civilisation beneath a winter moon. Soon he would be with Sallie who, they'd told him, was frantic. He was desperate for the sight of her, the smell of her, wanting to hold her in his arms…

She heard his key in the lock a second before the phone rang. Ignoring its strident interruption, she flew down the stairs and into his arms. For an endless moment they stood entwined in the bliss of being together again, shaken by the depth of their feelings. When she looked up she was weeping and he said softly, 'Don't cry, Sal. I'm not worth it.' At that the tears flowed faster.

'Hey,' he chided. 'I'm back, safe and sound. Slightly frostbitten, very grimy and dying of hunger.'

'People have died up there in this kind of weather,' she choked. 'I thought that was what was going to happen to you, and I'd never told you that I love you now more than ever. I love you for the way you've tried so hard to make up for what you did. For the way you've put up with my coldness towards you. For the way you are such a clever, caring doctor.' She was smiling now. 'And because you are still the most wantable, attractive and sexiest of men.'

His smile was brighter than the sun. 'Is that so?' he breathed. 'As soon as I've got rid of the grime, I'll see if I can live up to that.'

'Yes!' she whispered. 'Just don't ever leave me again, Steve.'

'I won't! Be assured of that! When I came crawling back I was so desperate to be near you I would have lived in a tent in the garden if you'd refused to have anything to do with me, rather than return to the life I'd been living.'

The police rang while he was getting cleaned up. It seemed that it had been them earlier when she'd flung herself downstairs at the sound of the key being turned in the lock. When the officer at the other end of the line heard the lift in her voice he said, 'So you've got your husband back, Dr Beaumont. Safe and sound, I'm told.'

'Yes, thanks,' she said. 'I am so grateful to all of you who helped to find him.'

'The mountain rescue boys are the ones to thank for that,' she was told.

'Yes, I know, *and* people like the young constable who called here this morning at five o'clock.'

'He was just doing his job,' was the reply. 'Like your husband was when he went to visit his patient. Thankfully he came to no harm, mainly because he did the right thing by taking shelter and staying put until the weather calmed down. Where is he now?'

'Under the shower,'

'Right. I'll leave you to it, and a merry Christmas when it comes.'

Christmas! she thought as she put the phone down. It had been the last thing on her mind over the last two days, but in less than a week it would be here and she still didn't know where Melanie was going to live.

'You remember the little jaunt I'd promised you?' Steve said when he reappeared.

'Yes, of course I do. Though I have to admit that it hasn't been uppermost in my mind in view of the fact that you've been missing for twenty-four hours. Christmas hasn't been on my mind either, until the police rang a moment ago to say that you were safe. The officer I spoke to wished me a merry Christmas and suddenly it hit me how near it was.'

'Yes, well, it will be time to concern ourselves about Christmas when this other thing is sorted.'

'I'm hoping that it's connected with Melanie,' she told him. 'Because if it isn't, it's going to be a bit cramped in here over the festive season.'

'It is connected with her,' he admitted as he tucked into the food she'd put in front of him, 'but only in a roundabout sort of way. As it's Saturday tomorrow, there'll be all the time in the world for me to explain what it's all about.'

'This project that you're doing with some of the men from the village—is Jack Leminson involved in it?'

He stopped eating and raised his head. 'Why do you ask?'

'He was at the surgery with a whiplash problem and was asking if you'd taken me to see something or other that sounded as if it might be the same thing.'

'And what did you say?'

'Not a lot. I just let him see that I was more concerned about you being missing than some village matter that will, no doubt, sort itself. Tonight we have more important things to attend to.'

He was on his feet with the plate empty, and, taking her in his arms, he said softly, 'Haven't we just.'

She was laughing up at him. 'I'm referring to *me* tucking *you* up in bed for a few hours while you recover from your ordeal. You look exhausted.'

'Nothing of the kind!' he protested.

She stroked the strong lines of his face with gentle fingers and saw the desire in his eyes that only she had ever kindled. 'I'd like you to be at the peak of your prowess when we make love for the first time in an eternity,' she teased.

He pretended to shudder. 'Don't mention that word. I've had my fill of peaks during the last twenty-four hours. I don't care if I never see another.' He paused and his expression grew serious. 'On the subject of those majestic piles, what about Jennifer? I'll have to follow that up tomorrow. When the ambulance came for her I impressed on them that she wasn't to be sent home in the present weather conditions. I believe the elbow was fractured, so I did the right thing sending her to A and E. But everything would have been so much simpler if I hadn't locked up her house and given her the key. I could have sheltered at her place until the blizzard was over.'

'So ring the hospital first thing in the morning,' she

suggested, 'and now go to bed, Steve. I'll still be here when you wake up.'

'All right,' he agreed, 'but on one condition.'

'And what's that?'

'When I've made love to you, we have the ceremony of slinging out the shirt. It has served its purpose. When you need something to hold onto in the night, I'll be there…for ever and always.'

He came to her at dawn, as she'd sensed he would. So dear was he to her heart that the tears came again. Without speaking, he put a finger to his lips and carefully wheeled Liam's cot into the other room. Then he came back to stand beside the bed and as he looked down at her in the early morning light he asked, 'Are you sure about this, Sal? I've waited a long time for it and so have you. I can wait longer if I have to.

'You said yesterday how much you loved me, but you were overwrought and overwhelmed with relief when I turned up. It wasn't the right time for such declarations. You could be having regrets by now.'

She raised herself up and, reaching out for him, pulled him down beside her and told him softly, 'My only regret is that it's taken me so long to start living in the present, instead of letting the past bog me down. You and I were always meant for each other, but somewhere along the way we took a wrong turning, and the magic went. Do you think we can find it again?'

'Yes. I know we can,' he said as he took her in his arms.

And later, much later, after they'd been to the stars and back and she was cradled in the crook of his arm, Sallie knew that he hadn't been wrong.

When Steve turned into Bluebell Lane later and stopped the car beside Henry's cottage, Sallie said, 'Henry's away at his daughter's.'

'Yes. I know,' he said calmly. 'We're not here to see Henry.'

Liam was behind them in the baby seat and as Steve reached in and undid the strapping he said, 'Have you noticed that the house next door is finished?'

'Yes, so it is!' she exclaimed, getting out of the car. 'I haven't been this way for a while. It's beautiful, isn't it? And uncanny the way it has all the features that I would have chosen.'

Steve smiled. 'It isn't uncanny,' he said. 'It's been planned. The house is ours, Sallie. This is where I've been coming in the evenings to check on progress. When we looked at the plot that day and you told me what kind of a house you would build on it if it was yours, I decided that was what it was going to be— yours and mine.'

He hesitated before continuing. 'The only thing that has taken the pleasure out of watching it take shape has been the thought that you might have drifted so far away from me that you wouldn't want to live here.'

So far she hadn't spoken. She'd just listened opened-mouthed to what he'd had to say, but now she found her voice and as they walked through the gates and slowly up the drive she said, 'I can't believe it, Steve. That you would go to all this trouble for just a whim of mine. It's the most beautiful thing you've ever done for me and I'm glad we had those fantastic moments this morning before I saw it. So that you know how much you mean to me, no matter what you do.'

'Talking about places to live, has anything occurred to you?' he asked.

'No. Should it?'

'I said I'd found somewhere for Melanie to live, didn't I?'

'Of course!' she cried. 'They can have the apartment.'

'Yes, they can.' Putting his hand in his pocket he pulled out a bunch of keys. 'Welcome to your new home. Dr Beaumont, and if you'll give me a moment while I put this young man back into the car seat, I'll carry you over the threshold once you've unlocked the door.'

As Sallie went from room to room, entranced with everything she saw, Steve told her, 'I haven't done anything about furnishings except for having carpets put down. I thought you would want to choose everything else yourself. If we go into the town this afternoon and smile nicely at some of the staff in the furniture stores, who will not be busy because everyone is out buying presents, we should be able to get the basics delivered before Christmas.'

'I don't mind if we have to sleep on the floor,' she said dreamily. 'I feel as if we've come out of a long dark tunnel.'

'We have,' he said, eyes darkening, his voice tender,

and she knew he was remembering what had happened in the winter dawn. They had come together with such passion and joy she'd thought she would burst with happiness, and now there was this, too, this wonderful house that Steve had had built for her.

Before Steve had had a chance to ring the hospital that morning Jennifer had come on the line to say that the snow ploughs had been out and cleared the way to her house and she was now back home with a carer in attendance.

He hadn't been too pleased to hear it, having asked the authorities to get in touch with him before they did any such thing, but when he'd protested she'd said, 'I'm to blame for that. When they told me you'd been trapped on the moors, I was appalled and told them that you were not to be bothered after such an ordeal. So I'm home now. The arm is in a cast. They had to operate, by the way, and I've got a carer coming up from the village from nine to five every day.'

'So you are all right?'

'Yes, I am, and guess what? The vicar came to see me when I was in A and E. He was there visiting somebody else and saw me arrive. I've asked him to call when the snow has gone about me starting a drama class in the village hall. I'm beginning to feel as if I belong after all, and the three of you can take credit for that, you, your lovely wife and the vicar. But most of all you, Dr Beaumont. You're a good man.'

As he'd replaced the receiver Steve had been smiling. 'She is some woman, that one. She's home, with her arm in a cast, and has sorted out a carer from the village to come in every day as she didn't want to bother me after what happened to me. But wait for it, most surprising of all, she's going to start a drama group in the village.'

'So she has a heart after all,' Sally had said delightedly.

Jack was back to see Sallie about his aching neck, or so he said, but she had a feeling that it was really to find out what she thought of the house.

'It's delightful,' she told him. 'The most wonderful surprise. I believe you had orders not to tell anyone who it was for while it was being built.'

He grinned at her from the other side of the desk. 'Sure did. I told your husband that his wife was a lucky woman to have that sort of a surprise being arranged for her. For my part, building a lovely house for you made me feel a bit better over the way our young Cassandra behaved that time.'

'That's all in the past,' she told him. 'She's turned out a fine young woman, and as for myself, yes, I am fortunate, very fortunate indeed. Steve and I got lost along the way and it was an awful time for both of us. But finding each other again has been so wonderful it has made up for what went before.'

'Good for you,' he said, then added, 'So, about my neck.'

'Is it better or worse?'

'It's about the same, painful.'

'Maybe a course of physiotherapy is called for.'

'Sure. Anything that will make me fit for the job. I might be the boss but I do my share of the heavy work.'

Melanie and Rick were due to fly into Manchester Airport early on the morning of Christmas Eve, and after days of non-stop activity the two doctors and the baby had moved into their dream house to leave the apartment ready for their arrival.

Steve was going to the airport to pick them up before morning surgery, and Sallie knew that he would be giving the new man in his niece's life a critical once-over.

They had cared for Liam devotedly and, knowing Steve, he wouldn't be happy to let him be transferred into the care of someone he thought unsuitable, whether Melanie was the mother or not.

Neither of them had slept on the night before their arrival because ever since the day Steve had come back to where he belonged there had been a family feeling in the apartment and they'd both revelled in it, each of them loving Liam equally.

But now that part of their lives was over. It was time to hand him back to his mother, which was right and proper. No more cuddles and baby smiles or tender moments when they watched him lovingly as he slept.

As Sallie tossed and turned restlessly Steve took her in his arms and said consolingly. 'There is one good thing, Sal. At least we'll be able to watch Liam grow up. He'll be where we can see him as the years go by, instead of being somewhere far away.'

She nodded sombrely. 'Yes. I know we should be

glad that we'll have that to hang onto. I always knew it would be like this when we had to give him up but, Steve, I wouldn't have wanted to miss looking after him for Melanie. Would you?'

'No, of course not. He was the extra little bit of icing on the cake when you let me come back into your life.'

And now the moment they were dreading in one way and looking forward to in another had arrived. As Sallie opened the door of the apartment, they were coming up the stairs with the eager young mother in the lead, followed by the new man in her life and Steve bringing up the rear.

She saw that he was smiling and a quick glance at the stranger supplied the answer. Rick Martinex was tall, with blue eyes and shoulder-length blond hair, yet it was his smile that Sallie noticed first. A broad, friendly beam that was immediately reassuring.

But it was Liam in his play-pen who took centre stage. He'd just learned how to pull himself upright by holding on to the bars and was watching what was going on with big eyes.

When she saw him, Melanie burst into tears. 'Oh, Sallie,' she sobbed. 'He's so big and so beautiful! How can I thank you both?'

'You could let us babysit, or sometimes push him out in his buggy,' Steve said wryly, and Sallie swallowed hard. She could feel the familiar pain around her heart. It was always there when she thought of their childlessness. But this was *their* moment, Melanie's and Rick's, and she didn't want to cast any gloom around.

Unaware of her momentary melancholy, Steve was saying to the young couple, 'Welcome to village life. There's nothing to beat it. If you don't mind, I have a job to do, taking the last surgery before Christmas. Sallie is going to give it a miss this morning, but one of us has to be there.'

When he had gone downstairs she said, 'It's so lovely to see you both here safe and well. Steve has had a house built for the two of us, so the apartment is yours, if you want it.'

'That's great!' Melanie cried, and Rick thanked Sallie profusely.

'I've written down Liam's routine,' she told them. 'It will take him a while to get used to you and he might cry for us sometimes. But if his daily routine stays the same for the time being, he should be all right, and I'm just down the road if you need me.'

'I've stocked the fridge and changed the sheets and I'm now going to pick up the turkey that I've ordered from the butcher, while you get to know your son again, Melanie. We're expecting the three of you to join us for Christmas lunch, if that's all right with you. We're looking forward to getting to know you, Rick. I hope you'll be happy here.'

As she drove to the new house, after doing the last of her food shopping, Sallie was thinking that she should be content, knowing that the young couple had arrived safely and were adequately provided for with accommodation and food. But the knowledge that their time with Liam was at an end was going to hurt in days to come.

He was where he ought to be now, with his mother, and she'd no quarrel with that, but it was still hard to let go and she knew that Steve was going to feel the same.

Melanie was going to have to take it slowly with her little one. So far the three people he'd bonded with had been Steve, Hannah and herself. His mother and her partner were going to have to do some bonding of their own.

When she turned into Bluebell Lane her spirits lifted as the house came into view. It was still hard to believe it was theirs until she put the key in the lock and stepped inside. Living and loving in this beautiful house was paradise. It was the kind of home she'd always dreamed of, with fields and the river close by. When they lay in each other's arms in the night they could hear it bustling along on its never-ending journey to join the mighty Mersey.

She and Steve were back to how they'd once been, older and wiser maybe but with their delight in each other restored. Life was perfect It was as if all the clouds but one had disappeared from their sky and she wasn't going to dwell on that.

The first time she'd seen the house she'd been able to picture children frolicking in the garden and sleeping in the bedrooms, but it seemed as if that would never be. Not their children anyway. But as long as they had each other again they were going to take each wonderful day as it came and be thankful.

* * *

Christmas morning in the new house was magical. There were presents waiting to be opened beneath the tree, the turkey was in the oven and a flash of bright colour on the river bank announced the presence of a kingfisher. Up above a flock of geese swooped and swirled in formation on their way to the further reaches of the river.

Soon Melanie and Rick would arrive with Liam for Christmas lunch and the day would be complete for the two doctors whose most precious gift to each other was a love that had been battered but not broken.

There were changes in some people's lives after Christmas. Melanie took on a part-time receptionist's position at the surgery and Rick was working for the local estate agent, and with his easy charm was proving to be the right man for the job.

Still with her arm in a cast, Jennifer started the drama group the first week in January with the vicar's blessing, and was amazed to find how popular it was.

Any change in Philip Gresty's life had to be for the worse. He was much less well than he'd been at Janine's wedding, and whenever Steve visited him he was humbled by his friend's acceptance of his lot.

The district nurse and the physiotherapist visited regularly, but there wasn't a lot they could do, except for the nurse to help him with bathing and the physio to arrange some gentle exercises.

Dale had taken over the running of the farm and

Anna and Janine spent their time caring for Philip and keeping the riding school and shop functioning.

And then there was Liam. There'd been a big change in his life and for a while he'd been fretful, missing Sallie and Steve, but with regular visits from them, and the short memory of children of his age, he was adjusting, with lots of love from his mother.

CHAPTER NINE

THE days of bliss came to an end when one morning Steve found some kind of body change in the place he'd been operated on. It wasn't a lump exactly, but there was something there.

'I knew it was too good to last,' he groaned as he came out of the shower.

'What do you mean?' Sallie asked, quite unprepared for what was coming next.

'I think the cancer might have come back. I can feel something there.'

'Oh, no!' she breathed.

'Oh, yes, I'm afraid,' he said tightly. 'I've been clear for three and a half years and now, when life is so wonderful, this happens.'

It was a Sunday morning, so getting in touch with Tom Cavanagh would have to wait until the following day, and for the rest of the weekend it was like sitting on a knife edge, with Steve not saying much but being just as loving as ever, and Sallie praying that he was wrong.

Thankfully they'd moved on since the last time,

she was thinking. He wouldn't let it get to him like it had before. For one thing, he would be much more aware of the seriousness of the situation if the cancer was back, although Tom had assured him that he was in full remission, and so had oncologists he'd seen in other places.

When Steve phoned Tom on Monday he wasn't there. He'd gone away for a long weekend and wouldn't be back until the following day, and Steve thought that they were having a taste of being on the other side of the fence again, relying on the medical profession and hoping it wouldn't let them down as they waited for him to return.

Sallie wasn't feeling very well herself. She'd felt tired of late and had had a couple of gastric upsets. They'd had staffing problems at the practice since the Christmas break, which had increased the workload for Steve and herself, and she'd put it down to that.

One of the practice nurses had left to go into hospital work and a receptionist had gone to look after elderly parents in Cumbria. The good thing about that was it had left a gap for Melanie to slot into, but she was having to be trained, as was the new practice nurse they'd appointed, and it all took its toll.

Sallie decided that she must have been overdoing it and was going to slow down. But the feeling of being less well than usual had seemed like nothing when Steve had stepped from under the shower on that January morning after the alarming discovery.

Tom Cavanagh was smiling when Steve walked into

his consulting rooms to keep an appointment that had been hastily arranged.

'So how long have you been back in these parts, Steve?' he asked.

'A few months,' he told him. 'I couldn't keep away from Sallie any longer, Leaving her was the most stupid thing I've ever done, and coming back was the most sensible. She and I are closer now than we've ever been. We've just moved into a fantastic house by the river, and life was wonderful until I felt what might be the return of the cancer.'

Tom didn't ask him if he'd fathered any children. He knew it would have been the first thing Steve would have told him if it had been the case. 'I'm glad you are back together,' he said. 'You two were made for each other. So where is Sallie now?'

'Holding the fort at the practice. Whatever is happening in our lives, there are still two surgeries a day to deal with and home visits to carry out.'

When he'd finished his examination Tom said thoughtfully, 'I'm not sure what I think. There is something there, but it could be a lesion, scar tissue from the operation. Obviously we're going to have to go through the tests routine again before I can give you an answer.'

'And if the cancer *has* come back?'

'Let's not jump to conclusions. I'll set the tests up for tomorrow. It will be more or less a repeat of last time.'

As Sallie dealt with her Tuesday morning surgery, she had herself under control, knowing that she would be doing herself or her patients no favours if she didn't keep her mind on the job. But once surgery was over, the queasiness she'd felt ever since Steve had left for his appointment became worse, and as she got up from her desk the room began to spin round and she crumpled onto the carpet.

Steve returned at that moment and found her there, and as he bent over her anxiously he thought bleakly that this new development was taking its toll on Sallie.

She opened her eyes and when she saw him looking down at her she groaned. 'I must have fainted,' she said, raising herself to a sitting position. 'Some use I'm going to be if I'm wilting around the place when you need my support. What did Tom have to say?'

'He's not sure. The usual tests are being set up for tomorrow. But at the moment I'm more concerned about you.'

'You needn't be. I'm all right,' she protested, as he helped her to her feet. 'My nerves were in knots all the time I was seeing the patients, and I think the effort of trying to keep calm must have been too much. Oh, Henry Crabtree was here. He's moving back into his cottage tomorrow,' she said with a weary smile, 'and is delighted to know we're his new neighbours. His comment was, "So I can just pop across if I'm under the weather, then."'

'We're going to have to put him right about that, I'm afraid,' Steve remarked dryly. 'And now you are going home to rest while I take over for the remainder of the day.'

'Not until I've had a peep at Liam first. Hannah has just brought him back from the shops.'

'I'll join you for that. It's so good that we can still see him whenever we want to.' Lowering his voice in case Melanie was around, he said, 'Not a word to Melanie or anyone else about what is going on in our lives until we get the verdict.'

Steve had been for the tests and all they could do now was wait for a phone call from Tom. Each time Sallie gazed around the house that Steve had had built for them she wanted to weep. She loved the place, but without him there beside her it would be empty and meaningless.

After finding her in the faint he'd insisted that she give the surgeries a miss for the rest of the week, and, though reluctant to do so, she'd agreed. Having time on her hands, though, made the waiting seem longer.

That night as they ate their evening meal Steve noticed her pallor and wondered if she was ill and not telling him because she didn't want to put any more burdens onto him. Whatever it was, he knew there was something wrong. He could feel it in his bones.

Later, as they lay in bed, holding hands and listening to the river running past, his anxieties were still there, and when he turned to take her in his arms he saw that she was asleep.

As he looked down at her in the moon's light, she looked pale and ethereal and his unease increased. He'd been the one with the health problems so far. Was it going to be Sallie's turn now?

His innards were clenching at the thought of anything

being wrong with her. It would be the first time if there was, but the cancer had been the first time he'd had anything wrong with him. Which said that years of good health were nothing to go by if nature had some trick up its sleeve.

During the rest of the week Sallie pushed Liam out a couple of times in his buggy and enjoyed every moment, but once she'd returned him to his doting mother the days seemed to stretch for ever.

It wasn't warm enough to sit out in the garden in January's chill, and when she'd done any household chores she wandered aimlessly from room to room, wondering how much longer before Tom had news for them.

It was to be soon. On the Friday morning Steve had just finished the home visits when the call he'd been waiting for came through. Knowing that what Tom had to say in the next few seconds could put an end to his and Sallie's hard-won happiness, he braced himself for what was coming.

'You're clear!' Tom's voice said in his ear, quietly exuberant. 'It *was* scar tissue and everything else is fine. You're going to live to fight another day, my friend.'

'Thank God!' Steve breathed. 'I can't wait to tell Sal.'

'Go and do it, then,' the other man advised laughingly, and Steve didn't need to be told twice.

Back at the house and desperate for something to do, Sallie was unpacking some of the clothes she'd brought with her from the apartment, and had just unearthed the dress she'd worn on their first date years ago. She'd kept it for sentimental reasons and was suddenly tempted to see if she could still get into it.

Of pale apricot silk, with a long skirt and boned bodice, it was no longer fashionable, but she would always treasure it. As she slipped it over her head it was tight and the boned bodice was like a vice. With a grimace she took if off and felt her breasts where the bodice had been.

They were really tender, and with cancer being the only thing she and Steve had been able to think about for days, she was suddenly uneasy, and sank down onto the nearest chair to think about it.

Tender breasts, nausea, tiredness, fainting—all might be signs of it, but they were also signs of something else. Pregnancy! Ever since they'd first tried to start a family, she'd kept a note of dates, but because of all that had happened in the last weeks before Christmas and her anxiety over Steve since then, every other thought had been driven from her mind.

She opened her diary with trembling fingers, and it was there. The date when her last period had been due. As her heartbeat quickened and her mouth went dry, she saw that it should have been three weeks ago.

To someone who had never been late in her life, it had to mean one thing. Unless it was due to the shock of what was happening to Steve. There was only one way to know for certain and within minutes she was on her way to the chemist's.

The test showed positive! She couldn't believe it and

the tears began to fall. They'd waited all this time and now when Steve's life might be threatened, they were going to have the child they longed for.

She'd imagined countless times how it would be if she ever told him she was pregnant. There would be joy, delight and every triumphant emotion she could think of to mark the occasion. But it wouldn't be like that if he was going to get the thumbs-down from Tom. Life could be so cruel.

When his car pulled up in the drive shortly afterwards she knew he'd got the results, even though his expression gave nothing away. He came into the house with his usual brisk stride and called her name, and as she went into the hall to meet him he picked her up in his arms and danced her round and round.

'It was scar tissue,' he cried. 'I'm clear, Sal. The way ahead is just as we want it to be. Being aunt and uncle to Liam, looking after the village and living and loving in our beautiful house.'

'With our children,' she said in breathless wonder.

He frowned. 'I think not,' he said. 'But one can't have everything in this life, and thank God I've got you!'

She was smiling up at him from his arms. '*You* think not. I think so.'

'What do you mean?'

'I'm pregnant.'

'What?' he exclaimed, putting her slowly back on to her feet.

'I'm a doctor, for heaven's sake! But because my mind has been so full of what has been happening in our lives over recent weeks, I haven't been checking my dates. Otherwise it might have occurred to me that I was showing all the signs of pregnancy instead of thinking I was run down.'

'But are you sure?'

'Mmm. I've been to the chemist.'

There was a smile on his face the like of which she'd never seen before.

'We've been given two life lines in one day,' he rejoiced. 'I'm OK and we are going to have a child. Do you think it was conceived the night I came home after being lost on the moors?'

'There have been other occasions since,' she told him laughingly

'Yes, but that time was in a class of its own.'

'Yes. It was indeed.'

'A child of our own at last!' he choked. 'Wait until Melanie and Rick hear this. They'll be so glad for us, and so will the village.'

'Could we keep it to ourselves for a while?' she asked. 'You know how we've talked about a house-warming. I thought we could have one in a couple of weeks' time, and tell everyone our wonderful news then. All those we care for will be there. Melanie and Rick with Liam, Hannah, Alison and the vicar with their boys, Philip and Anna Gresty, if we can somehow manage to get him here, and how about Jennifer, if she'll come?'

'That's a great idea,' he said enthusiastically, 'but you'll have to keep me gagged until then. I feel like doing the town crier bit and going around the village, announcing to everyone our fantastic news. Have you thought of any names?'

'Steve!' she exclaimed laughingly. 'I'd only just found out when you arrived. There will be plenty of time for that.'

'Mmm,' he murmured with his arms around her. 'Time for everything, and only a few hours ago I thought there was going to be time for nothing.'

Later that day they phoned Colin in Canada, feeling that of all people he should be told their good news. Colin had been the one who'd brought them back together and they owed him a lot.

Sallie spoke to him first and he was delighted to hear her voice. 'How are you and Steve getting along?' he asked.

'We are back together in every sense of the word,' she told him happily, 'and we have you to thank for that. We've moved into a beautiful house that Steve has had built for us in Bluebell Lane. But, Colin, the main reason I'm phoning is to tell you that we are going to have a baby. I'm pregnant, and you can imagine what Steve is like. He's over the moon. We only found out today and aren't telling anyone locally yet. But we both feel that you should be the first to know.'

'That is wonderful news!' he cried. 'Wait until I tell Jessica.'

She passed the phone to Steve and his first words were, 'So, Colin, what are the chances of you both coming over for the christening? How would you feel about being one of the baby's godfathers?'

'The answer to both questions is yes,' he said. 'Yes, we will come for the christening and, yes, I would love to be a godfather.'

When they'd said goodbye Sallie was smiling. 'Aren't we being a bit previous, arranging such things? We are several months away from the event. Anything could go wrong.'

'No way,' he said. 'I'm going to cherish you like you've never been cherished before.'

They'd planned the house-warming for early February and all those invited had been pleased to accept, including their new neighbour, Henry Crabtree, Lizzie Drury and Jack Leminson and his wife.

'I think old Henry has his eye on Mrs D.,' Steve said as they dressed for the occasion.

'Surely not,' she said laughingly. 'Lizzie Drury would never fancy Henry.'

He was zipping up the long strapless dress she was wearing and brushed his lips against her bare shoulder. 'You didn't fancy me second time round, did you?' he teased.

'Oh, yes, I did,' she protested, swivelling to face him. 'I never stopped fancying you. But it took the thought of losing you to bring me to my senses.'

She touched his face with gentle fingers. 'Shall we go and prepare to greet our guests?'

'Of course. I've been waiting for this moment ever since that wonderful day when you told me I was going to be a father.'

When all the guests had arrived and been served with drinks, he said, 'Sallie and I have arranged this house-warming for two reasons—first of all because we want to welcome you all to our new home, and secondly because we have some fantastic news. Sallie is pregnant. We are going to become parents.'

He went across the room to where his friend was slumped in a wheelchair. 'Do you hear that, Philip?' he said softly. 'We are going to have a baby.'

It had been an effort for the sick man to get to the party, but he had made it and there were tears in Philip's eyes. 'Wonderful!' he said, bringing the word out with difficulty, and after that there wasn't a dry eye in the room.

It was September, harvest time again. The windberries were ready for picking, and as the farmers celebrated the yield of their fields once more, Sallie and Steve were excitedly awaiting the birth of their babies. She was carrying twins and they were due any day.

Life ever since that day when Steve's burden had been lifted off him and Sally had found she was pregnant had been a time of happy amazement that had reached new levels when a scan had shown that there were two babies in her womb. They didn't know the sex. Didn't want to. It was enough to know they were there.

There had been only one dark cloud in the sky during

those months of contentment. Philip had died in the early summer, and much as he was mourned by his family and friends, there had been none who would have wanted to see him suffer any longer.

During her pregnancy Sallie had worked part time at the practice. They'd taken on a trainee GP, the son of a retired doctor in the next village, and he was proving to be a good choice.

After those first few weeks of lethargy and nausea she had bloomed like a flower in the sun, and as he watched over her Steve could scarcely believe that soon there would be two babies in the house by the river.

'Pregnancy suits you,' he'd told her smilingly one day, placing his hand on her bulge. 'We've come a long way since the day I told you I had cancer, haven't we? From having no family, we'll soon have two children.'

'And maybe more,' she'd said, laughing up at him.

'I saw Tom Cavanagh the other day,' he'd told her, 'and he was highly amused to know that I'd fathered twins when I had such grave doubts about even fathering one child. How about asking him to be one of the godparents?'

'Yes,' she'd said immediately, 'and there is Melanie and Anna, and what about Jack, who built our lovely house for us? I have a feeling that he would be pleased to be asked.'

'Fine by me,' he'd said, 'All we need now is the safe arrival of the babies.'

'I'll second that,' she'd told him softly.

* * *

Stephen Philip Beaumont and his sister Lauren Elizabeth came into the world on a golden September morning, and as Sallie lay back and observed Steve with a baby in each arm, it was as if all their lives they had been waiting for this moment.

MILLS & BOON®

Live the emotion

NOVEMBER 2006 HARDBACK TITLES

ROMANCE™

The Italian's Future Bride *Michelle Reid*	0 263 19262 8
Pleasured in the Billionaire's Bed *Miranda Lee*	0 263 19263 6
Blackmailed by Diamonds, Bound by Marriage *Sarah Morgan*	
	0 263 19264 4
The Greek Boss's Bride *Chantelle Shaw*	0 263 19265 2
The Millionaire's Pregnant Wife *Sandra Field*	0 263 19266 0
The Greek's Convenient Mistress *Annie West*	0 263 19267 9
Chosen as the Frenchman's Bride *Abby Green*	0 263 19268 7
The Italian Billionaire's Virgin *Christina Hollis*	0 263 19269 5
Outback Man Seeks Wife *Margaret Way*	0 263 19270 9
The Nanny and the Sheikh *Barbara McMahon*	0 263 19271 7
The Businessman's Bride *Jackie Braun*	0 263 19272 5
Meant-To-Be Mother *Ally Blake*	0 263 19273 3
Falling for the Frenchman *Claire Baxter*	0 263 19274 1
In Her Boss's Arms *Elizabeth Harbison*	0 263 19275 X
In Her Boss's Special Care *Melanie Milburne*	0 263 19276 8
The Surgeon's Courageous Bride *Lucy Clark*	0 263 19277 6

HISTORICAL ROMANCE™

Not Quite a Lady *Louise Allen*	0 263 19060 9
The Defiant Debutante *Helen Dickson*	0 263 19061 7
A Noble Captive *Michelle Styles*	0 263 19062 5

MEDICAL ROMANCE™

The Surgeon's Miracle Baby *Carol Marinelli*	0 263 19098 6
A Consultant Claims His Bride *Maggie Kingsley*	0 263 19099 4
The Woman He's Been Waiting For *Jennifer Taylor*	
	0 263 19517 1
The Village Doctor's Marriage *Abigail Gordon*	0 263 19518 X

MILLS & BOON®   1006 Gen Std LP

Live the emotion

NOVEMBER 2006 LARGE PRINT TITLES

ROMANCE™

The Secret Baby Revenge *Emma Darcy*	0 263 19014 5
The Prince's Virgin Wife *Lucy Monroe*	0 263 19015 3
Taken for His Pleasure *Carol Marinelli*	0 263 19016 1
At the Greek Tycoon's Bidding *Cathy Williams*	0 263 19017 X
The Heir's Chosen Bride *Marion Lennox*	0 263 19018 8
The Millionaire's Cinderella Wife *Lilian Darcy*	0 263 19019 6
Their Unfinished Business *Jackie Braun*	0 263 19020 X
The Tycoon's Proposal *Leigh Michaels*	0 263 19021 8

HISTORICAL ROMANCE™

The Viscount's Betrothal *Louise Allen*	0 263 18919 8
Reforming the Rake *Sarah Elliott*	0 263 18920 1
Lord Greville's Captive *Nicola Cornick*	0 263 19076 5

MEDICAL ROMANCE™

His Honourable Surgeon *Kate Hardy*	0 263 18891 4
Pregnant with His Child *Lilian Darcy*	0 263 18892 2
The Consultant's Adopted Son *Jennifer Taylor*	0 263 18893 0
Her Longed-For Family *Josie Metcalfe*	0 263 18894 9
Mission: Mountain Rescue *Amy Andrews*	0 263 19527 9
The Good Father *Maggie Kingsley*	0 263 19528 7

MILLS & BOON®

Live the emotion

DECEMBER 2006 HARDBACK TITLES

ROMANCE™

Taken by the Sheikh *Penny Jordan*	0 263 19278 4
The Greek's Virgin *Trish Morey*	0 263 19279 2
The Forced Bride *Sara Craven*	0 263 19280 6
Bedded and Wedded for Revenge *Melanie Milburne*	
	0 263 19281 4
The Italian Boss's Secretary Mistress *Cathy Williams*	
	0 263 19282 2
The Kouvaris Marriage *Diana Hamilton*	0 263 19283 0
The Santorini Bride *Anne McAllister*	0 263 19284 9
Pregnant by the Millionaire *Carole Mortimer*	0 263 19285 7
Rancher and Protector *Judy Christenberry*	0 263 19286 5
The Valentine Bride *Liz Fielding*	0 263 19287 3
One Summer in Italy... *Lucy Gordon*	0 263 19288 1
Crowned: An Ordinary Girl *Natasha Oakley*	0 263 19289 X
The Boss's Pregnancy Proposal *Raye Morgan*	0 263 19290 3
Outback Baby Miracle *Melissa James*	0 263 19291 1
A Wife and Child To Cherish *Caroline Anderson*	0 263 19292 X
The Spanish Doctor's Convenient Bride *Meredith Webber*	
	0 263 19293 8

HISTORICAL ROMANCE™

The Wanton Bride *Mary Brendan*	0 263 19063 3
A Scandalous Mistress *Juliet Landon*	0 263 19064 1
A Wealthy Widow *Anne Herries*	0 263 19065 X

MEDICAL ROMANCE™

The Surgeon's Family Miracle *Marion Lennox*	0 263 19100 1
A Family to Come Home to *Josie Metcalfe*	0 263 19101 X
The London Consultant's Rescue *Joanna Neil*	0 263 19519 8
The Doctor's Baby Surprise *Gill Sanderson*	0 263 19520 1

MILLS & BOON®

Live the emotion

1106 Gen Std LP

DECEMBER 2006 LARGE PRINT TITLES

ROMANCE™

Love-Slave to the Sheikh *Miranda Lee*	0 263 19022 6
His Royal Love-Child *Lucy Monroe*	0 263 19023 4
The Ranieri Bride *Michelle Reid*	0 263 19024 2
The Italian's Blackmailed Mistress *Jacqueline Baird*	
	0 263 19025 0
Having the Frenchman's Baby *Rebecca Winters*	0 263 19026 9
Found: His Family *Nicola Marsh*	0 263 19027 7
Saying Yes to the Boss *Jackie Braun*	0 263 19028 5
Coming Home to the Cowboy *Patricia Thayer*	0 263 19029 3

HISTORICAL ROMANCE™

An Unusual Bequest *Mary Nichols*	0 263 18921 X
The Courtesan's Courtship *Gail Ranstrom*	0 263 18922 8
Ashblane's Lady *Sophia James*	0 263 19077 3

MEDICAL ROMANCE™

Maternal Instinct *Caroline Anderson*	0 263 18895 7
The Doctor's Marriage Wish *Meredith Webber*	0 263 18896 5
The Doctor's Proposal *Marion Lennox*	0 263 18897 3
The Surgeon's Perfect Match *Alison Roberts*	0 263 18898 1
The Consultant's Homecoming *Laura Iding*	0 263 19529 5
A Country Practice *Abigail Gordon*	0 263 19530 9